Susan L. Pare

THE ~~POOP~~ *Proof*

IS IN

THE PUDDING

MORE BY THIS AUTHOR

Blueberries and Bears and My Brother's Shoes

Red, White, and Blue (A Short Story)

She Never Stopped Talking

Red

The House on Ludington Street

What's Behind the Screen Door?

The Mayor's Son

Willerton Woods

Cowtown

Floating Face Down
A Sheriff "Cowboy" Berkson Mystery Novel – Book Three

Let's Play Autopsy

A Bad Week In Hollister
A Sheriff "Cowboy" Berkson Mystery Novel – Book Two

Don't Smother Your Mother
A Sheriff "Cowboy" Berkson Mystery Novel – Book One

Crossing Sydney

Index

DEDICATION

Patty V.
Steve T.

Thank you for being my eyes.

"I have everything we need except for the brandy and a package of chopped pecans," Charlotte told her granddaughter, Marla Jo. "I'm sorry, sweetie. It looks like I'm going to have to run to the store. Plus, I need a bottle of wine."

Slightly confused, Marla Jo glanced at the recipe. "I don't see wine listed in this recipe. What do you need that for?"

"To drink, of course," Charlotte replied, smiling. "There's nothing like having a few glasses of wine while you're making bread pudding."

"I guess that's one ingredient that goes into you and not the pudding," Marla Jo said, laughing.

"I've never made bread pudding without drinking a little wine. In fact, I usually have wine no matter what I'm cooking. I guess that's what makes me such a good cook. Both me and the late Julia Childs," Charlotte said grinning.

"I thought the secret to being a good cook is to make your guests wait to eat until they are practically starving. By then, anything will taste good."

"That, too. Well, girl, it looks like we're going to have to put this lesson on hold until after I go to the store."

"Darn it, Grandma. I was really looking forward to learning how to make your pudding."

"Me, too. I'm sorry I didn't check to see that I had everything we needed before you got here. But, we'll do it real soon." Charlotte looked at Marla Jo, who was reaching for her purse. "Are you leaving already?" she asked, obviously disappointed.

"I'm sorry, Grandma, but if we aren't baking today I should go to work. I've got this case I've been working on that needs my attention. I'll call you later."

"Maybe, we can get together tomorrow. I'll go to the store this afternoon and pick up the stuff we need."

"Sorry, love, but tomorrow's not good. I'll let you know when I have some free time again." Marla Jo picked up her purse, kissed her grandmother goodbye, and headed for the door. "See you soon."

"See you, too," Charlotte called out. "Call me."

Marla Jo turned and looked at her grandmother. "I almost forgot. Mom wants to know if you're coming over for dinner on Sunday. It's dad's birthday."

"I'll let her know," Charlotte replied curtly.

"Grandma, you have to get over it. I'm sure dad is sorry for what he said."

"I am not a whore, Marlie. Just because a woman is married more than once doesn't make her a whore. Or, to quote your father - a slut. That's what he called me, you know."

"He was drunk. He didn't know what he was saying. Can't you just get over it for mom's sake?"

"He's always drunk. Your mother should kick his sorry ass out the door. She's put up with his crap for years. Well, I don't have to listen to it. So, unless your father apologizes for what he said to me, I don't care to be in the same room with him."

"Mom will be awfully disappointed if you're not there."

"She'll get over it," Charlotte said.

"Grandma, why don't you be the bigger person? You know how much dad loves your bread pudding. Why don't you make some and bring it with you on Sunday?"

Charlotte stared at her granddaughter, thinking about what she had said. "Your father doesn't deserve my pudding."

"Come on, Grandma."

"Well, I guess it would be the Christian thing to do," she commented after a few moments. "I'll think about it. How about that?"

"Please come."

Charlotte sighed. "All right. You know I can't say no to you. But, he better keep his nasty remarks to himself."

Smiling, Marla Jo hugged her grandmother. "You're the best, Grandma. See you Sunday," she said, as she ran out the door.

Marla Jo called her secretary, Joyce, from her car and informed her that she was on her way to the office.

"The phone has been ringing off its hook," Joyce told her. "You have gobs of phone calls to return and there is a Mr. Richard Stiverson on his way in to see you."

"I thought you told me that I don't have any appointments this morning."

"You don't. I told him you weren't here and that he needed to make an appointment. He refused to make one. He said he was on his way and he would wait until you got here."

"The name doesn't ring a bell," Marla Jo said. "Who is he?"

"He's the husband of the late Barbara Stiverson. Rather, I should say, he's the ex-husband of the late Barbara Stiverson."

"Did he say what it was about?" Marla Jo inquired.

"It seems that the late Mrs. Stiverson has numerous life insurance policies with our company. He informed me that he is the beneficiary of at least two of them," Joyce stated. "He wants his money."

"This is not ringing a bell at all," Marla Jo told her. "I'll be there shortly. Pull Mrs. Stiverson's file. I want to review it before I talked to the man. Put him in the waiting room if he shows up before I get there."

"Will do. And, just so you know, Mrs. Stiverson was murdered."

"How come I'm only hearing about this now?"

"Probably, because she was only killed yesterday."

"Yesterday? And, he wants his money already?"

"Some people don't know how the system works. Hold on. Phone's ringing."

Marla Jo ended the call and pulled into her parking spot. "I really have to talk to her about putting me on hold," she muttered, as she got out of her car.

Marla Jo threw her jacket on a chair, walked over to her desk, and pushed the intercom button on her phone. "Joyce, see if you can get in touch with Detective Robert Donovan."

"You're here," her secretary said, surprised. "I didn't see you come in."

"I came in the back way."

"Oh. How come?"

"Just try to get in touch with Donovan, will you?" Marla Jo said, ignoring Joyce's inquiry.

"By the way, is Donovan still working out of the 3rd Precinct?" Joyce asked.

"He is. If he's out, leave a message asking him to call me back as soon as possible," Marla Jo told her.

"Mr. Stiverson is in the waiting room. Should I send him in?"

"Not yet. I want to talk to Donovan first."

Marla Jo looked down at the open file on her desk. It contained six life insurance policies, which were dated from 1997 to 2018. Except for the policy listing Faith Church beneficiary, all of them were for substantial amounts of money.

"Marla Jo?" Joyce called over the intercom.

"Yes."

"Donovan's not there. I left a message."

"Fine. You can show Mr. Stiverson in."

Marla Jo didn't look up as Stiverson entered her office. She waited until he was almost to her desk, then looked up at him, and smiled. "Please, have a seat. I'll be with you in a moment," she said, motioning to the chair in front of her desk.

Stiverson glared at her as she continued glancing through the insurance policies. After a few moments, he coughed.

"I know you're there, Mr. Stiverson," Marla Jo told him. "I'm just about through here."

"I'd like to get at this," Stiverson said. "I haven't got all day, you know."

Marla Jo looked up at him. "It's unusual for someone to keep paying for an insurance policy with an ex-spouse as the beneficiary. Usually, once the marriage is over, the policies are canceled."

"Is that right?"

"It is. May I ask why your ex-wife didn't cancel these two policies?"

Stiverson shrugged. "It's no big deal. It was part of our divorce agreement. She agreed to hang on to them as long as I reimbursed her for the cost of the premiums."

"I see."

"Ma'am, if you don't mind, I'd like my money. Who do I have to see around here to get a check?"

Marla Jo smiled. "Well, Mr. Stiverson, I'm afraid that isn't going to happen for a while. Your ex-wife was murdered and there's an investigation going on regarding her death. It is not our policy to release funds until the police have completed their inquiry. I'm sorry, but you are going to have to wait."

Stiverson's face slowly turned red as his anger level increased. "I didn't kill Barbara. I wasn't even in town when she was murdered. I want my money.'

"I'm sorry, but there's nothing I can do at this time. In fact, I'm not even sure if I'm going to be the one investigating this case."

"Listen, lady, I've got a couple of mil coming to me. I don't know what you think you're pulling but you guys are gonna pay me. Got it?" Stiverson yelled.

"I'm not trying to pull anything. This is standard procedure when someone has been murdered. You're just going to have to wait. Someone will keep you informed. Now, if there is nothing else. . ."

"You want me outta here? Fine but I'll be back, lady, and I'll be bringing my attorney with me," Stiverson shouted.

"Mr. Stiverson, you can yell at me until the cows come home but it isn't going to change anything. I'm sure your lawyer will explain that to you. And, I'd appreciate it if you would address me by my name and not lady. Good day, Mr. Stiverson."

Stiverson stood up and started walking towards the door. He turned suddenly and glared at the nameplate on Marla Jo's desk.

"Was there something else, Mr. Stiverson?"

"Marla Jo McKnight, is it? Your old man wouldn't be Frank McKnight, would it?"

"I'm sorry, but how do you know my father?"

"We used to enjoy a few drinks together down at Kelsey's."

"You used to?"

"Yeah, used to. No more, though. These days he gets pretty damn mean after a few drinks. I stay away from him when I can. Hell, most people do. Your old man can be a real bastard." He started walking closer to her desk.

"That's close enough, Mr. Stiverson." Marla Jo reached down and pushed a button located under the top of her desk. "I'd like you to leave. Now!" Marla Jo said, raising her voice.

"I'm going. Don't get your undies all in a bunch, lady," he said as he turned and started walking back towards the door. He gave Marla Jo a dirty look. "Yeah, you're Frank's kid all right. He's a prick and you're a real bitch." As Stiverson reached for the doorknob, the door swung open, hitting him in the face and knocking him backward.

"You have a problem here, Ms. McKnight?" Donald, the taller of the two security guards, asked Marla Jo.

"Yes, Donald. I'm having a little trouble getting Mr. Stiverson to leave my office. Perhaps you and Joe could escort him out of the building."

Stiverson, still shaky from being hit, held up his hands as he backed out of the room. "You lay one friggin' hand on me and I'll have you arrested."

"We're not looking for any trouble. We'd just like you to leave quietly," Donald told him. He glanced over at Marla Jo. "Is that all?"

Marla Jo shook her head yes. "Just get him out of here, please."

2

"Detective Donovan on line two," Joyce informed Marla Jo over the intercom.

"Thanks." As Marla Jo reached for the phone, she knocked over her soft drink. "Shit!" she exclaimed loudly. "Donovan, give me a second," she yelled as she picked up the phone. She grabbed a handful of tissues and soaked up the spilled drink. "Sorry about that," she said, as she put the phone to her ear.

"What's going on?" Donovan asked. "Are you okay?"

"I'm fine. I just spilled my drink. Have you got a minute?"

"For you? Always. So, what can I do for you this fine day?"

"Bobby, I have. . . I had a client that was murdered yesterday and I was wondering if you can give me some insight as to what's going on."

"Who are you referring to?"

"A woman named Barbara Stiverson. Are you familiar with the name?"

"Yeah. It's a fresh one. She was found dead late yesterday afternoon. How'd you hear about it? The newspapers just picked up on it this morning."

"Her ex showed up here a little while ago wanting his payout from her policies."

"Was it Richard Stiverson or Alfred Freemont?"

"Stiverson. Do you know him?" Marla Jo asked.

"He's a person of interest in this case. I was going to call you about this. I heard she had some life insurance policies with your company. Can you tell me how much money we're talking about?

"Barbara had six policies with us, Bobby. Stiverson is the sole beneficiary on two of them and they total a little over one and a half million dollars."

"Holy crap. Well, that puts him at the top of my list. Can you give me an idea of what else you're dealing with? Who are the beneficiaries of the other policies and what are they worth?"

"Just a sec," Marla Jo flipped through the file and pulled out the six policies. "Ready?" she asked Donovan.

"Ready."

The first policy was taken out in 1997, naming Stiverson beneficiary and its face value is $800,000.00. The second one, also naming Stiverson, was taken out in 1998. That one is for $750,000.00.

"That's a nice windfall," Donovan observed. "They got divorced in 1999. I wonder why she kept the policies."

"I asked him. He said it was part of the divorce agreement. He agreed to make the premium payments if she wouldn't cancel the policies."

"What about the other four policies?"'

"One for Bella Francis and one for David Freemont. They are her kids and each gets $500,000. She took these two policies out in 2013."

"And, the other two?"

"Faith Church is listed on one and it's for $25,000.00. She took that out last year. No, nix that one. She canceled it before it became effective." Marla Jo stared at the sixth policy, not believing her eyes. "Wow!" she exclaimed. "Well, this is very interesting."

"Whatcha got?" Donovan asked.

"A one million dollar policy that was written in 2013. Alfred Freemont is. . ."

"Alfred Freemont? Are you sure?" Donovan

interrupted. "They divorced in 1986."

"I'm sure. What the hell, Bobby. Why would she take out a policy twenty-seven years later and name her ex-husband beneficiary?"

"Do you know who has been paying the premiums on that one?"

"It looks like she has but Freemont could have been reimbursing her. I'm going to have to subpoena her financials," Marla Jo told him. "This is very suspicious."

Donovan didn't respond.

"Are you still there?" Marla Jo asked.

"That's over three and a half million dollars, M. J. I had no idea your company would write that large an amount for one individual."

"Some of these policies were written over twenty years ago. Things have changed a lot since then, but it's still all about the premiums, you know."

"Can you send me copies of those policies?" Donovan asked.

"I can."

"Thanks."

"You know, there's a good possibility that she might have had more policies with other insurance companies," Marla Jo declared. "Have you checked with her attorney?"

"We're looking into it."

"Is this your case, Bobby?"

"Yeah, I've been assigned to work it."

"Do you have any idea who did it?"

"Not right now, I don't. I thought we had a pretty good idea, but the list of suspects just got a lot longer."

"How was she killed?" Marla Jo asked.

"It was a brutal, nasty murder and it was up close and personal. I'd definitely say it was someone she knew."

"So, was she stabbed or shot or what?"

"God, M. J., do you really need all the gruesome details?"

"Yes, please."

"Well, then, yes."

"Yes, what?"

"It looks like she was stabbed, although. . ." Donovan took a breath. "This was probably the worst crime scene I've ever seen. We're still going through the house looking for missing pieces. Happy now, you pervert?"

"What do you mean, looking for pieces? Pieces of what?"

"What do you think I mean?"

"Oh, God, no," Marla Jo said after a few seconds. "Why would you tell me that?"

"Seriously, M. J.?"

"I'm sorry I asked. Okay?"

"So, are you the investigator for this case?" Donovan asked.

"We just found out about it. It hasn't been assigned yet, but I'm gonna ask for this one. I've met Stiverson and he's a real piece of work. Just from what I've seen today, I'd lay odds he did it."

"Hold on there, M. J. You have to keep an open mind."

"I know. I was just saying, is all. When do you plan on talking to her attorney?"

"Sometime today."

"You'll keep me informed?"

"Of course. Don't I always?" Donovan replied.

"Okay, I've got to go. The boss is in and I'm going to go talk to him."

"Let me know if you get the lead on this one. Okay?"

"Will do. Bye, now."

Marla Jo hung up the phone and sat back in her chair, thinking about her conversation with Donovan. "I'd lay odds it was an ex," she uttered. "I just wonder which one."

Twenty minutes later, Marla Jo was back at her desk. It hadn't taken much to get her boss to agree to her heading up the Stiverson case. She picked up the phone and called Detective Donovan's cell phone.

"Donovan here," he answered abruptly.

"I got it," she exclaimed.

"Good to hear. I'm busy. We'll talk later."

"What are you doing tomorrow?" she asked before she realized that he had already ended the call.

"I only have a minute, Mom. I just wanted to let you know that grandma will be there Sunday, but she's still upset over what dad said to her."

"I know. I talked to her."

"You've got to make him promise to be on his best behavior."

"I'll tell him, but you know your father. He gets a few beers in him and that mouth of his takes over his brain. I can't control him, you know that."

"Just tell him that grandma is making her bread pudding for him and if he doesn't behave he won't get any."

"I'll mention it."

"And, he needs to apologize to her for calling her a slut. That was so out of line," Marla Jo said.

"I know, but you have to consider the source."

"I don't know why you put up with it."

"I really don't care to have this conversation again, Marlie."

"I know. Sorry. I've got to go. I'll talk to you later. Bye."

"Bye."

3

"It is my opinion that Mrs. Stiverson knew she had cancer before she made an appointment with me. While we were going over her health history, she told me that a few years ago she spent the summer in England. She informed me that she became ill and had to see a doctor. I believe she was told, at that time, that she had cancer."

"Do you think it's possible that she came home and didn't tell anyone?" Marla Jo asked.

"I believe that might be the case. However, I must add that if this was the case, she never expressed it to me personally. It is just my opinion."

"Why do you feel she already knew she was sick?"

"The lack of emotion she had when I informed her that her tests were positive. She didn't shed a tear or even get a little bit upset. That's not what I normally see when I tell a patient that they have cancer. I had the feeling that it was not a surprise to her."

"When was the first time you saw her for this condition?"

The doctor glanced at his computer screen. "It was in September of 2015. I ordered tests to be run and I saw her two weeks later to give her the results. That was the last time I saw her."

"If she knew she had cancer. . . Well, do you think she wanted a second opinion?"

"No. I think she wanted a referral."

Marla Jo studied the doctor's face. He was probably in his early fifties and extremely good-looking. She glanced at his left hand and noticed a wedding ring. "And, by then, she had already taken out more insurance,"

Marla Jo stated.

"If you say so," the doctor said. "I'm shocked that she lasted as long as she did. Normally, with this type of cancer, life expectancy is not that long."

"Your office must have been contacted by our company for her health records."

"I wouldn't know. You can check with the front office and see if that ever happened."

"Doctor, you have her file right in front of you on your computer. Could you take a look, please?"

"Ms. McKnight, we recently updated our software. This type of information would not have been included. As I said, you'll have to check with the front office."

"I gather that you didn't treat her for her cancer?"

"No. I'm not an oncologist. I said I thought she was looking for a referral. I referred her to Dr. Steven Lockley. He's the one you should be talking to. However, I'm not entirely sure she ever made an appointment with him."

"Wouldn't he have followed up with you if she had seen him?"

"That would be the proper procedure but I don't recall hearing from him. Although, with the software update, it's possible that information wasn't transferred over from her past records. You might want to check that out with the. . ."

"front office," Marla Jo interrupted, smiling.

"Exactly." The doctor frowned and glanced at the computer screen. "That's all the information I can give you. Now if there's nothing else. . ." He looked over at her.

Marla Jo made a notation in her notebook and closed it. She stood up and reached across the doctor's desk to shake his hand. "Thank you for your help. I may be contacting you again if I have more questions."

Ignoring her outstretched arm, the doctor looked up at her and frowned. "I hope that won't be necessary."

Marla Jo pulled her arm back, picked up her purse, and walked out of his office. "What a dumb ass," she muttered, as she closed the door.

"Who's a dumb ass?"

Marla Jo turned and grinned when she saw Detective Donovan walking towards her. "What are you doing here?"

"Probably the same thing as you. How'd it go?"

Marla Jo shrugged. "That doctor has the personality of a wet fish. However, that's beside the point. It seems that the doctor thinks Barbara knew she was dying years ago. If that's the case, we could have some serious insurance fraud here, Bobby. I bet you anything that she took out some of those policies after she knew she had cancer."

"Good luck proving it," Donovan said.

"I've got my work cut out for me with this one, that's for sure."

"I think we both do. I'm seeing her attorney when I leave here. Do you want to wait and go with me?"

Marla Jo hesitated for a moment. "I'd like to, but I've got an appointment at. . ." She glanced at her watch. "It's not as late as I thought. I'll wait for you. I'll be in the Coffee Shop downstairs. Come find me when you are done with Mr. Personality."

"Boy, he sure got under your skin," Donovan commented.

Marla Jo smiled. "I guess, maybe a little. But, he is a prime example of that old saying that you can't judge a book by its cover."

"Detective Donovan, nice to meet you," Murray Levinson said as he shook Donovan's hand. "Please have a seat." Murray Levinson glanced over at Marla Jo. "Ma'am. Have a seat, please."

"This is Marla Jo McKnight. She's an investigator for The Second Century Insurance Company," Donovan told him.

Marla Jo shook Levinson's hand. "Nice to meet you."

"So, you two decided to gang up on me," Levinson said, grinning.

"I'd say you're killing two birds with one stone," Donovan said, laughing. "I ran into Ms. McKnight, told her I had an appointment with you, and asked if she'd like to join me. I figured we might as well save you the trouble of having to talk to us individually."

"That's mighty thoughtful of you." Levinson sat back in his chair and stared at Donovan. "Well, what can I help you with?" he asked after a few seconds.

"Mrs. Barbara Stiverson."

"Ah, yes. Terrible thing, what happened to her. Do you have any leads, Detective?"

"I'm working on it. I gather you are also the executor of her estate."

"I am."

"What I need to know is who the beneficiaries of her estate are. I assume you have a copy of her Will."

"I do. Although, I'm slightly hesitant to give out that information yet. I'd like to wait until after the reading of the Will."

"And, I'd oblige you, except this is a murder case, Mr. Levinson, and time is of the essence. So, if you don't mind – well, I'd like to know what's in it."

"Of course." Levinson opened a thick file and flipped

through the documents. "Here's Barbara's Will." He opened it and started to glance through it. "I'll make you a copy, Detective. However, I'd appreciate it if you would give me time to inform her family of its contents before you share this information with anyone."

"Agreed," Donovan replied.

"The main beneficiaries are her son, David, and her daughter, Bella. She bequeathed some money to her church and except for a few minor donations, that's it."

"Did she leave anything to Alfred Freemont or Richard Stiverson?" Donovan asked.

"Just a few personal items, but no money."

"Well, there's nothing suspicious about her Will," Marla Jo commented. "You do have copies of her life insurance policies, don't you?"

"Yes. They are right here," Levinson said, as he reached for a stack of documents on his desk. He grinned. "Now, it gets interesting."

"How so?" Marla Jo asked.

"Let me read you the list and the amounts. Then, you tell me."

"You can skip the ones with my company. I just need to know if there are any more."

He sat up straight in his chair and flipped through the policies, setting aside the ones with The Second Century Insurance Company. "It looks like your company isn't the only one Mrs. Stiverson dealt with," Donovan commented. "There are four more policies."

"So, she did take out more policies," Donovan commented. "Who gets what?"

"Her brother, Roger Harper, $500,000.00; her sister, Janet Harper Fisher, $250,000.00; Mary Johanson, her housekeeper of over twenty years,

$75,000.00; and, finally, Alex Morris, her health care provider, $250,000.00." He removed his glasses and sat back in his chair.

"That's a lot of money for a lot of people," Donovan said as he looked at Levinson. "I'd appreciate it if you could make copies of everything and get it to me at the 3rd Precinct."

"I'll see to it. Is there anything I can do for you, Ms. McKnight?"

"I'd also like a copy of the Will. And, copies of the life insurance policies that weren't written by my company, if you don't mind."

"No problem," Levinson said, smiling. "I'd appreciate it if you keep me appraised of how the case is going, Detective."

"I will."

"I don't envy you," Levinson declared.

"Why's that?" Donovan asked.

"Because you have a lot of people who are going to be foaming at their mouths wanting their money and one of them might have killed her. You've got your work cut out for you."

"True. Of course, no one is collecting anything from the estate until this case is tied up."

"If you don't mind my asking, Mr. Levinson, do you have a rough idea of how much Mrs. Stiverson's estate is worth?" Marla Jo asked.

"Including all her properties, cash, savings, personal items, and so on, I'd say a rough guess is around ten to twelve million dollars."

"Not including the insurance," Marla Jo added.

"Not including the insurance," Mr. Levinson confirmed.

"I don't envy you either, Mr. Levinson," Donovan said, as he pushed his chair back and stood, getting ready to leave.

"And, why is that, Detective?"

"Because, once you read that Will and the beneficiaries find out that they have to wait for all that money, they'll be all over you like white on rice."

4

They were hungry. He wished he had put more meat into the plastic bag before he had left the woman's house. It was that damn siren that had scared him and made him run out the back door. It was only a frickin' ambulance but he figured it best if he took off and stayed satisfied with what he had.

He looked over at Charlie and sighed. Poor fellow. He was old and he didn't know how much longer Charlie would be around. He knew he couldn't afford to take care of him much longer. The thought of Charlie dying brought tears to his eyes. They had been partners for a long time now and once Charlie was gone he would be alone.

He walked over to a small grime-covered refrigerator and opened it. He looked inside, hoping to find that a miracle had taken place and he would find something to eat.

"Damn it," he yelled as he slammed the door shut.

Charlie opened his eyes and looked over at him.

"Sorry, old boy, I didn't mean to wake you. I'm going out for a while. Maybe the butcher has an old ham bone or something he will give me so I can make some soup. If not. . . Well, don't you worry none. I'll find something for us to eat."

He reached for an old tattered sweater lying on the bed and put it on. He checked his pants pocket to make sure he had his keys and pocket knife and walked towards the door. "I'll be back in a bit," he said, as he walked out of the small one-room apartment.

5

Marla Jo stood on the sidewalk in front of Levinson's building and glanced around. "Traffic's a bitch today," she muttered.

Donovan glanced over at her, frowning. "What did you say? I couldn't hear you."

"Forget it." She looked at her watch to check the time. "I've got to get going," she declared. "I'm already late for an appointment. Call me if you find out anything." As she turned and started walking towards her car, Donovan grabbed her arm.

"Wait a minute," he yelled, hoping to be heard over the sound of a city bus driving past them.

Marla Jo stopped walking, turned back, and smiled at him. "What is it?"

"How about dinner tomorrow night? Or, are you busy?"

Surprised by his invitation, she thought for a moment, wondering what brought this on. "I think I'm free, but let me check my calendar when I get back to the office. I'll give you a call," she told him.

"I thought it would give us a chance to discuss the case. You know, compare notes."

"Well, crap, Donovan. Here I thought you were asking me out on a date and you just want to talk business," she said, grinning. "I guess I've lost my charm."

Donovan smiled. "How about we do both? We could have a nice meal somewhere and talk. And if the subject of Barbara Stiverson comes up – well, then, we can talk about her, too. I think the autopsy has been completed and, if you want, I'll share the results with you."

"Now how could I turn that down?" Marla Jo replied. "How about picking me up around seven?"

"Sounds good," Donovan replied.

"And, Bobby?"

"Yes."

"Let's go casual. Nothing fancy. Okay?" she asked. "I get tired of being dressed up all the time."

"Jeans casual or khakis?"

"Wear what you want but I'll be in jeans and a sweater," she told him. "Seriously, I've got to get going. I'll see you tomorrow."

Donovan watched her as she walked to her car, got inside, and drove away. Man, he thought, it wouldn't take much to. . . "That was probably a mistake," he muttered to himself, grinning.

Marla Jo was ready to call it a night. Her appointment had rescheduled and she was tired. Tomorrow was Saturday and she had made an appointment for a haircut and a manicure. She was looking forward to going to dinner with Bobby and she wanted to look her best.

Joyce knocked once on the door to Marla Jo's office and opened it.

"What is it?' Marla Jo asked.

"Do you need me for anything else?" Joyce asked.

"Nope. Go on home and enjoy your weekend."

"You, too," Joyce replied. "Are you doing anything special this weekend?"

"Actually, I am. I'm having dinner with Detective Donovan tomorrow night and dinner at my folks' house on Sunday. It's my dad's birthday. How about you?"

Joyce grinned. "You're going out with Donovan, huh? I went out with him a few times, you know."

"Really?" Marla Jo said, looking surprised. "You've never mentioned that before."

"No reason to. He's a nice enough guy but we didn't click. It turned out that we had nothing in common. Besides, he's a little too old for my taste."

Marla Jo grinned. "I can see that. What are you anyway? Twenty-five?"

"Just about. I'll be twenty-five on January first. I was a New Year's baby."

"That's pretty cool," Marla Jo stated. "Well, have a good weekend. I'll see you Monday."

"Right, Boss. Bye," Joyce said, as she left Marla Jo's office, closing the door behind her.

Marla Jo sat back in her chair, frowning. "What the hell? Bobby went out with Joyce?" she muttered.

Hearing the doorbell, Marla Jo glanced at her watch. "He's early," she muttered. She tightened her robe around her, walked to the door, and swung it open. "Damn it, Donovan, you're half a. . ." She stopped talking and looked up at a very tall man standing in her doorway. "You're not Donovan," she stated.

"No, I'm not. Are you Marla Jo McKnight?"

"Who's asking? 'Cause if you're selling, I'm not buying."

"I'm not selling." He reached into his pocket, pulled out a large envelope, and handed it to her. "This is for you." As Marla Jo reached across the threshold and took the envelope, the man grinned. "Consider yourself served," he said, as he turned and walked away.

"Wait a minute," Marla Jo yelled. "What is this for?"

The man looked back at her, waved, and kept on walking. "I serve them. I don't read them, lady. That's your job."

Marla Jo stepped back inside her house and shut the door. "Shit!" she exclaimed. "I should know better than to open the door to strangers." She glanced at the envelope. "To hell with it," she muttered and threw the envelope on the coffee table. "It can wait."

At exactly seven o'clock the doorbell rang. This time Marla Jo checked to see who it was before she opened the door. "Bobby, you're extremely punctual. Good for you."

"I don't believe in keeping a woman waiting." He looked her up and down and grinned. "You look great," he told her. "Those jeans look. . ."

"What?" Marla Jo stepped back and stared at him. "Too tight?" she asked. "Maybe I should change."

"Don't you dare," Donovan said. "I was kidding. You look exactly right. Are you ready?"

"Let's go," Marla Jo replied, grabbing her purse from off the couch. "Where are we going?"

"I thought Boomer's Bar and Grill would fit the attire for the evening. Have you been there?"

"I have and I love it. An excellent choice, Bobby." She made of point of checking him out and smiled.

"Do you like what you see?" he asked.

"Oh, ya. You look pretty good yourself. Only, maybe your jeans could be. . ." She grinned.

"What?" Donovan asked, looking concerned.

"I don't know. Maybe just a little tighter," she told him, laughing.

6

"Oh, my God, this has to be the best burger I've ever eaten," Marla Jo told Donovan.

"You know you're not supposed to talk with your mouth full, don't you?"

"I can't help it. I don't want to stop eating long enough to talk."

Donovan laughed. "Well, I'm glad you're enjoying it. Although, if you don't stop moaning, people are going to wonder what I'm doing to you under the table."

Marla Jo laughed. "I wasn't moaning, you jerk."

"The hell you weren't. Anyway, before you crammed that burger in your mouth, you said you don't know why you were served a subpoena. How could you not look at it?"

"I was busy and it will still be there when I get home. I figure it's a relative of some policyholder suing to get a share of the money. It happens, you know."

Donovan watched as Marla Jo stuffed the last bite of her burger into her mouth and chewed it up. He grinned. "God, I love a woman who enjoys her food. Most of the women I date order a salad because they're watching their weight and are afraid they are going to gain an ounce."

Marla Jo wiped her mouth and looked across the booth at him. "Speaking of the women you date, Donovan. I was. . ." She hesitated.

"What?"

"I understand you used to date my secretary."

Donovan looked confused. "Who?"

"My secretary Joyce. She told me you guys went out

a few times."

"I dated your secretary? I don't think so. What's her last name?"

"Walters."

"Joyce Walters is your secretary? I'll be damned. I had no idea."

"She said she cut it off because she thought you were too old for her."

Donovan grinned. "Is that what she told you? I was too old?"

"That's what she said. She thought you wouldn't be able to keep up with her," she told him grinning.

"I never dated your secretary, M. J.," Donovan said, totally serious now. "If she told you we dated, she's lying through her teeth"

"I don't get it. Why would she tell me that?"

"I have no idea why. If I recall right I met her at a function I attended. It was a charity thing that the police were. . ." He sat back and frowned. "Now I remember. She came on to me. She had a little too much to drink and she made a pass. I sidestepped and that was that." He shook his head. "I had totally forgotten about that. In fact, I didn't even know that she was your secretary."

Marla Jo grinned. "Well, it looks like she remembers you."

"Her problem, not mine."

"It's kinda my problem now."

"Why would you think that?" Donovan asked.

"I have a liar working for me. I won't put up with that. She'll have to go."

"Well, then, that is your problem," Donovan said, grinning.

"Do you want dessert?" Marla Jo asked, changing

the subject.

Donovan stared at her and laughed. "You're kidding. Right?"

"Not at all. I hear they make a fantastic lava cake here and I'd like to try it."

"Then, lava cake it is," Donovan said, motioning to their waiter to come over to their table.

"So, you don't have a cause of death?" Marla Jo commented, a half-hour later. She looked down at her empty plate.

"You're not going to pick that plate up and lick it, are you? " Donovan asked her, chuckling.

"Don't be a smart ass. So, no cause of death?" she asked again.

"No. Although, my guess is that she was stabbed. Or, strangled. It's impossible to tell with some of her parts missing, M. J. The coroner managed to piece most of her back together, but the heart, liver, and part of her left arm is missing."

"What do you mean, part of her left arm?"

"Her left wrist to the elbow is gone. We found her all over that house. It's the worst crime scene I've seen in my twenty years on the force."

"Do you think it was more than one person who killed her? It would almost have to be with that much damage, don't you think?"

"There's a good possibility that there was more than one person. We found a lot of fingerprints that we haven't been able to identify."

"Have you eliminated anyone as suspects yet?" Marla Jo asked.

"Actually, we have," Donovan told her. He took a sip

of his coffee and glanced at her."

"Well? Are you going to tell me who?"

"You really enjoy this, don't you?" he asked.

"Enjoy what?"

"All this murder shit."

Marla Jo looked away.

"Sorry," Donovan said. "I shouldn't have asked you that?"

"No. It's okay," Marla Jo told him. "You're right. Mysteries and murder shit fascinates me. I guess if I hadn't gone to work for The Second Century, I might have become a cop. Or, maybe a criminologist."

"No kidding," Donovan commented. "It's not too late you know," he told her smiling.

"You think so?" Marla Jo said, surprised. "Nah, I think it's way too late. Anyway, does that answer your question?"

"It does. And, I guess it's okay to tell you that we have eliminated several people as suspects."

"Who?"

"Well, Barbara's daughter, Bella to start. Also, her sister, Janet, and her housekeeper. Alfred Freemont is off the suspect list, and. . ." He thought for a moment. "The church, of course. That's it."

"So, half the list is gone. That leaves her son, one of her exes, her brother, and her health caregiver."

Donovan stared at her. "That was fast. What? You have the list memorized?"

"The insurance companies have to pay these people, Bobby. It's my job to know who is on your suspect list. It's also my job to find out when Barbara was told she had cancer. I'm pretty sure a number of the policies she had were written after she found out. We're talking big bucks here, you know."

"I do know. And, if I remember correctly, the only one who might collect on the insurance is Richard Stiverson. The rest of the policies were written after she saw that doctor back in 2012," Donovan said.

"Even so, you're still dealing with Barbara's Will, and her kids are the main beneficiaries. The insurance can't mean that much to David, so losing out on that is no big deal. He's inheriting a frickin' fortune."

"As is Bella," Donovan stated. "For all I know, she could have hired someone to kill her mother."

"David could have, too." Marla Jo said.

Donovan sighed. "I have an idea that this is going to take a long time to solve unless someone messes up or comes forward with some information. Someone has to know something."

"Have you had any other cases similar to this one? It could have been a total stranger who killed Barbara. Maybe, someone broke into the house and she caught them in the act. So, they murdered her."

"To be murdered the way she was had to have been personal. Someone hated that woman. A lot."

"I think you're right." She glanced at her watch to check the time. "Do you want some more coffee or should we get going?"

"Do you have someplace you need to be?" Donovan asked.

"Sorry. I've got an early appointment in the morning. I should get home and get some sleep."

"Oh," Donovan said, looking disappointed. "Well, then I guess we should leave."

"I had a great time, Bobby. Perhaps we can do this again sometime."

"I'd like that," Donovan told her. "So, what are you doing tomorrow?"

"It's my dad's birthday and my mom is having the family over for dinner. To tell you the truth, it's not something I look forward to. The last time we all got together, he called my grandmother a slut. He has a tendency to drink too much."

"Is there even one functional family living on earth?" Donovan inquired.

"Not that I know of," Marla Jo replied, grinning.

As they started to walk out of the restaurant, Marla Jo stopped and gave Donovan a weird look.

"What?" he asked her, starting to feel uncomfortable.

"What are you doing tomorrow?"

"Nothing special. Why?"

"How would you like to come with me?"

"To your parents' house? Oh, no. No, no, no. I don't think so."

"Come on. It will be fun. You can be my buffer. Maybe dad will behave and grandma won't have to kill him on his birthday."

Donovan shook his head no. "I don't think that's a good idea, Marla Jo."

She stared at him. "You just called me Marla Jo. I can't remember you ever doing that before."

"You might be right."

"How about I pick you up? Dinner is at five. They always eat early."

"It's not a good idea. . ."

"Good. It's settled then. Oh, Donovan, You're gonna have so much fun."

7

Detective Donovan was nervous, which was a strange emotion for him. But, for some reason, knowing he was about to walk into M. J.'s parents' house had him on edge. As he analyzed this feeling he wondered if he was concerned about making a good impression on her parents and, if so, why. Was it important to him because he had feelings for M. J?

"You're very quiet, Bobby? Is everything all right?" Marla Jo asked him as she pulled her car over to the curb and parked. She turned the ignition off, turned in her seat, and looked at him. "You're sweating. Are you sick?"

Donovan gave her a weak smile. "I'm fine."

"Seriously, if you don't feel good I can take you home."

"Don't be silly. I'm fine. I'm looking forward to meeting your family."

She studied his face for a few seconds and laughed. "Oh, my God. I don't believe it. Detective Robert Donovan is afraid to meet my family."

"I am not," Donovan protested. "I'm just trying to figure out what the hell I'm doing here, that's all."

"I'm sorry, Bobby. I didn't know this would make you so uncomfortable. I just thought you might enjoy a home-cooked meal while being entertained by a few crazy people." She turned the key in the ignition and started the car. "I'll take you home."

Donovan reached over and turned off the car. "You will not take me home. And, I'm not afraid of meeting your family. Let's go." He opened the car door, got out, and stretched.

Marla Jo got out and walked over to Donovan. "My parents' names are Frank and Betsy. Grandma is Charlotte but you can call her Grams if you want. My sister and her husband and their two boys will be here and my brother, Pete. He's divorced, so he'll probably be alone. Although, once in a while he brings a date."

"Got it," Donovan said. "What's your sister's name?"

"Suzie. Her husband is Mark and the boys are Mark, Jr. and Casey. Don't worry about talking to the kids. They will have their noses in their phones the entire time they are here."

Donovan took in a deep breath and let it out.

Marla Jo grinned. "Ready?"

"Piece of cake. Let's do it."

Donovan sat back in his chair and smiled. "That was, without a doubt, the best pot roast I have ever eaten, Mrs. McKnight."

"Betsy, please. I really would like it if you would call me Betsy. And, thank you for the compliment."

"Is there any more wine?" Frank asked his wife.

"I believe we drank it all. . ."

"I think I saw another bottle in the kitchen," Pete stated, interrupting his mother. "I'll go get it."

"I don't think we need any more wine, Pete," Betsy said.

"Go get it, Pete," Frank told his son. "What's it for, if not to drink? And, it is my birthday, you know. I think I'm entitled to another glass of wine."

Mark, Jr. grinned and poked his brother in his ribs.

"Stop it," Casey said, as he poked him back. "That's enough, you two," Suzie said. "Mother, next time, please remind me not to seat them alongside each other. I'm sorry, Robert."

Donovan smiled. "It's fine."

"Pete, I said get the wine," Frank demanded loudly.

"I think you've had enough to drink," Charlotte declared.

"And, my dear mother-in-law, I don't recall asking you for your opinion," Frank said sarcastically.

"You're the most obnoxious person I know.   Plus, you're nasty and rude. I don't know why Betsy doesn't. . ."

"Okay, Grams. That's enough. I think it's time for the cake and presents," Marla Jo interrupted. "How about it, Dad? Ready to open your gifts?"

Frank glanced over at Marla Jo and grinned. "Well, aren't you the little peacemaker?"

"I try, Dad," she told him.

Frank looked at his wife, who was sitting at the other end of the table and smiled. "Are there presents, Betsy?"

"Of course, Frank. It's your birthday. We always give you presents. Pete, would you go get your father's gifts?"

"And, don't forget that bottle of wine from the kitchen. Bring that, too," Frank yelled to Pete.

Donovan watched as Pete left the table and walked out of the room. "So, Frank, how many years are you celebrating today, if you don't mind my asking?"

Frank glared at him for a moment. "Who are you again?"

"Robert Donovan. I'm your daughter's friend," Donovan told him.

"What daughter?"

"M. J.," Donovan told him.

"M. J.? Who the hell is that?" Frank asked.

"Oh, God, no," Marla Jo muttered under her breath. "Here we go."

"Frank, I made you bread pudding for your birthday," Charlotte said, changing the subject. "Would you like some?"

Frank stared at her for a moment and then smiled. "I can't believe you made me my favorite dessert. I would love some." He looked at Betsy. "Go get it, will you? Have you ever had Charlotte's bread pudding, Robert?"

"No. I can't say I've ever had the pleasure," Donovan responded, amused that Frank now remembered his name.

"Well, you are in for a treat. Charlotte makes the best bread pudding in town. Isn't that right, Pete?"

"She sure does," Pete said, agreeing, as he placed the gifts and the bottle of wine on the table in front of his father.

"Suzie?" Frank said as he poured himself a glass of wine and took a big gulp.

"Yes, Dad."

"Don't you think your grandmother's pudding is the best?"

"We all do, Dad," Suzie said as she turned to Marla Jo grinning. "Don't we, Marlie?"

"We do indeed," Marla Jo agreed. "Mom, can I help you in the kitchen."

"No. You sit," Charlotte told her, as she stood up. "I'll help your mother get the pudding."

"Mom? Can I help with the coffee?" Suzie yelled to her mother who was in the kitchen.

"Stop yelling," Mark said softly.

"Sorry," Suzie said. She looked at her two sons and sighed. "Boys, would you like to be excused? I know you don't care for bread pudding"

"Sit!" Frank yelled as the two boys started to leave the table. "Everyone stays right here until we eat our pudding and you all sing happy birthday to me. And, watch me open my presents."

"Mom?" Casey asked, looking at his mother.

"Stay at the table, boys. I'm sorry that I forgot we still need to sing to Grandpa."

Betsy and Charlotte walked into the dining room, carrying the dessert and singing the Happy Birthday song. The family joined in as the pudding was served and applauded when they finished. Everyone yelled happy birthday and watched as Frank blew out the single candle that had been placed in the middle of his pudding.

"Remember, I get the first bite," Frank told everyone, making a show out of picking up his spoon and scooping up a huge amount of pudding. Everyone watched as he put it into his mouth and chewed. Suddenly, his expression changed and he spit the pudding out of his mouth onto the table.

"My God, Frank, what's wrong with you?" Betsy yelled.

"This tastes like shit!" he exclaimed, as he took a huge gulp of wine and swished it around in his mouth. He looked at Charlotte, who was watching him with a huge smile on her face. "What did you do, old woman?" he yelled.

"That'll teach you not to call me names, birthday boy," Charlotte shouted. "If you want to talk shit to me, then you can eat shit."

"What the hell are you talking about? I didn't call you nothing."

"You called me a slut. Remember?" Charlotte

grinned as she took a big spoonful of pudding and shoved it in her mouth. She looked around the table. "It's fine, everyone. Frank's the only one who is eating shit today."

"I'm gonna fucking kill you," he yelled at Charlotte.

"Dad, the boys. Watch your language," Suzie yelled.

"Language be damned," he yelled back as he scooped up a huge handful of his pudding and threw it at Charlotte. The glob of pudding flew past her head and landed on the wall in back of her.

"Missed me. You throw like a girl," Charlotte said, taunting him.

Glaring at Charlotte he stood up, knocking over the bottle of wine and spilling it all over the table.

"Oh, Frank, now look what you've done," Betsy cried out. "The wine is dripping all over the carpet."

Looking confused, Frank gaped at her for a second, grabbed the edge of the table to steady himself, and fell flat on his face.

Donovan jumped out of his chair and hurried over to Frank. He knelt down and felt for a pulse. He looked over at Marla Jo and shook his head no. "I can't find a pulse. Call 911." He checked again to see if Frank was breathing, determined he wasn't and started applying CPR.

"Oh, my God," Betsy yelled. "This can't be happening." She glared at her mother. "What did you do?"

Charlotte shook her head no. "I didn't do anything."

"Mother, what did you do?" she shouted again.

"It was a joke," Charlotte exclaimed. "I didn't know it would kill him."

"Grams," Marla Jo said softly. "What was a joke?"

"I put a little dog poop in his pudding," she told her, crying now. "It was just one little piece." She looked at

Betsy. "I got it from my neighbor's yard after her dog did his business. It's just a little dog and it wasn't very much. I didn't think it would kill him."

"So, his pudding actually did taste like shit," Mark said, grinning.

"Mark! This is not funny," Suzie said as the tears rolled down her cheeks.

"Pete, you know CPR?" Donovan called out.

"I do."

"Get over here and take over." He backed away from Frank's body to give Pete room to continue the compressions.

"I got it," Pete told him.

"All right, everyone but Pete. I want all of you to go into the living room. And, stay there. Nothing on this table or in the kitchen is to be touched. Understand?" Donovan told them.

He watched while Marla Jo's family walked into the living room. "M. J., stay here a minute, will you?"

Marla Jo looked at him, shaking her head in disbelief. "I can't believe he's dead."

"Do you think your grandmother is capable of poisoning him?"

Marla Jo stared at him. "How can you ask me that? You don't even know how he died yet. It was probably a heart attack." She wiped a tear out of the corner of her eye.

"Hopefully, that's what it was. But, do you?"

"Of course, she isn't," she finally told him. "She may have put dog poop in his pudding but she would never poison him."

"But, you did tell me earlier that Charlotte was mad at him."

"Mad at him, yes. But, not enough to kill him. Can you wait and see what he died from before you start laying the blame?"

8

Donovan checked the dining room table. He decided that all food samples had been collected for the lab to test. Then, he went to the kitchen and looked around, checking to be sure that nothing had been missed. The baking pan that had been used to make the bread pudding was on the counter. "Take the entire pan," he told one of the cops who were gathering evidence. "We want to make sure we check the rest of that pudding."

"Do you really think the old lady poisoned her son-in-law?" a tall, lanky cop asked him, as he dropped the pan into an evidence bag.

"I haven't a clue and right now I'm not about to speculate one way or the other. All I know is she said she put the dog poop in a plastic bag and brought it here in her purse. I guess she slipped it into his pudding when no one was looking."

"That's nasty," the cop commented.

"True dat," Donovan replied. "I sure as hell wouldn't want to get on her bad side."

"True dat, Donovan? Seriously?"

Donovan glanced over at the doorway and saw Marla Jo standing there watching him. "It just slipped out," he said as his face turned red. "I told you to stay in the living room. What are you doing in here?" he asked, changing the subject.

"We wondered if you're about through in here. Mom wants to make coffee and Suzie and Mark want to take the boys home. They figure that watching their grandfather die is enough trauma for today."

"I may need to talk to the boys but I guess I can do

that later."

"Why do you need to talk to them?"

"They are witnesses. However, I may not need to if the results of the autopsy come back that your dad died of natural causes."

"Which is probably the case," Marla Jo stated.

"I certainly hope so." He looked around the kitchen. "I think my boys are done in here," he told her. "Let's go talk to your family."

They walked into the living room and sat down. Donovan looked at Betsy and sighed. "I'm so sorry for your loss, Betsy. I know you're exhausted and would like me and my men to get out of your hair. It shouldn't be much longer. We're about done here. Right now, the rest of you may leave if you wish. I'll be in touch."

"I'm staying here with mom," Pete told him. He looked over at Charlotte. "What about you, Grams?"

"I think I'd like to go home," she said, her eyes red and swollen from crying.

"I think that would be best, Mother, considering what you did," Betsy said coldly, which made Charlotte cry even harder.

Donovan glanced over at Marla Jo with a questioning look on his face. "What's going on?" he mouthed.

Marla Jo reached over and took her mother's hand. "Mom, I want you to listen to me. Grandma did not kill dad. You're upset right now and you need someone to blame for what happened. Detective Donovan will check with the doctor to find out what happened to dad. And, you know – you know, in your heart, mom – that grandma didn't have anything to do with dad dying. So, stop being so nasty to her."

Betsy looked away, not saying anything.

"Mom? Did you hear what I said?" Marla Jo asked sharply.

Betsy slowly shook her head up and down. "I hear you," she replied. "You're right." She looked over at Charlotte and smiled. "I'm sorry, Mother. I don't know what got into me. Of course, you didn't have anything to do with Frank dying. You just fed him dog shit, that's all." She looked away trying to hold back a smile. Suddenly, no longer able to control herself, she started to laugh.

Donovan looked at Marla Jo, who was grinning from ear to ear. Charlotte looked at Betsy, surprised at her reaction, and started giggling. Suddenly, the whole family was laughing. He stood there with a stunned look on his face, surprised at the reaction to Betsy's comment. They are all either in shock or plain crazy, he thought.

"I wish I'd fed him shit years ago," Betsy declared, laughing even harder.

"You're welcome," Charlotte retorted, making everyone laugh even harder.

"M. J., may I see you in the dining room?" Donovan practically yelled over the commotion in the room.

Marla Jo looked over at him, her body shaking with laughter, and shook her head yes. She stood up and walked to the dining room.

"Yes?" she asked, trying to keep a straight face.

"What the hell is wrong with you people? Your father just died and you are all acting like you're at some kind of a celebration. What the hell, M. J.?"

Marla Jo took a deep breath and let it out, trying to get her control back. "I'm sorry."

"All right. So, you're sorry. That doesn't explain what is going on in that living room."

"A million emotions are being let loose. Okay? What's the difference if you laugh or cry, as long as you get it out of your system?" She sat down on a chair and looked up at Donovan. "Sit," she said, patting the chair next to her.

Donovan hesitated for a moment and then sat down next to her.

"The truth is. . ." She stopped talking and took another deep breath. "I don't think anyone is that upset that my father is dead, Donovan. He was not a nice man. He treated my mother like crap. He drank way too much and I'm pretty sure he hit her. No, not pretty sure. I know that he hit her. If I was my mother, right now, I'd feel like I had just been released from prison."

"Wow. I didn't know it was that bad," Donovan commented.

"Of course, you didn't. The thing is, we've been after mom for years to kick his sorry ass out. I loved my dad, Donovan, but he could be a real jerk."

"So, if it was that bad, I guess anyone of you had a reason to poison him," Donovan reflected.

Marla Jo stared at him. "You ass. Nobody killed him and stop thinking that or. . ."

"Or, what?" Donovan asked her.

"I don't know. But, you're way off base if you think one of us killed him. Now, can I give you a ride home?"

"Thanks, but I'm going to the police station."

"I could drop you off if you want."

"Thanks for the offer but I'll get a ride with one of my men.

"Bobby, I'm sorry."

"What are you sorry about?" he replied, looking confused. "You didn't do anything."

"I'm sorry I asked you to come here today. I knew it might get a little nutso, but I never expected all of this crap to happen." She grinned. "No pun intended."

Donovan shook his head. "Anyway, I doubt anybody did. Well, except maybe your grandmother. I figure she knew some crap would happen."

Marla Jo rolled her eyes.

"Don't roll your eyes at me. You said it first."

Marla Jo grinned. "True dat," she agreed.

9

"You're late," Marla Jo declared as Joyce walked into the reception area and hurried towards her desk.

"Sorry. Traffic was crazy this morning."

"Don't bother to take your coat off, Joyce. You won't be staying."

"How come? Do you need me to run to the store?"

"Your services will no longer be needed." Marla Jo told her as she held out an envelope. "This is your final paycheck, plus severance pay. Your personal belongings are in that box," she said, motioning toward a box that was on a chair. "Donald is waiting to escort you out."

Joyce looked shocked. "What the hell, Marla Jo? Don't I at least deserve some type of explanation? I don't understand what's happening here."

"I don't. . ."

"I get it," Joyce interrupted. "You're upset because I went out with Detective Donovan and now you want to get rid of me."

Marla Jo looked at her and shook her head. "Not at all. I'm upset because you didn't go out with Detective Donovan. Donald, would you please escort Joyce out of the building?" she called out.

Donald stepped into the room and picked up the box that held Joyce's belongings. "Let's go," he told Joyce.

"I don't understand," Joyce protested. "That doesn't make any sense."

"Think about it," Marla Jo said, as she turned and walked into her office.

"Bobby," she said, as she picked up the phone. "You tracked me down."

"I didn't think you'd be working today. How is your mom doing?"

"She seems to be holding up fairly well. I was going to spend the day with her, but she said that she and Pete were making all the arrangements and there is nothing she needs me to do. So, I decided to work on the Stiverson case."

"Have you found out anything?"

"As you know, Barbara Stiverson was in London in 2012. I've reached out to a business associate who works there to see if he can check the records and find out what doctor she saw."

"Would it be public records if she saw a private doctor?" Donovan asked.

"I'm not sure how their system works and it was seven years ago but he'll let me know. What about you? Any news on my dad?"

"Not yet."

"Well, at least you're waiting before you arrest my family for murder."

"Be nice, M. J."

"Sorry."

"I'm bringing in Barbara Stiverson's brother and her caretaker for interviews this afternoon. I was wondering if you'd like to sit in."

"I'd love to. What time?"

"You need to understand that you can only listen and not ask questions."

"I know," Marla Jo replied. "Of course, I'll need to talk to them later, along with the other two that don't have alibis."

"Stiverson and her son, David," Donovan stated.

"Exactly. So, what time?"

"Around one-thirty. Can you make it?"

"I'll be there," Marla Jo told him.

"Do you want to do lunch first?" Donovan asked her.

"Sorry, I can't. I'm going to run over to mom's and make sure she's okay.

"Of course. All right, then, I'll see you later."

Roger Harper topped out at approximately five feet two inches tall. He dyed what little hair still remained on his head a flaming red, which he pulled back and fastened like a ponytail. It would be kind to say he was butt ugly.

Marla Jo walked into the interview room and sat down next to Donovan. She pulled a notebook and a pen out of her purse and laid them on the table in front of her.

Donovan looked over at her and smiled. "Good to see you, M. J."

"You, too," she replied.

"I'd like you to meet Mr. Roger Harper, Barbara Stiverson's brother."

"How do you do," Marla Jo said.

Harper looked at her and shrugged. "All right, I guess," he mumbled.

"Mr. Harper, this is Marla Jo McKnight. I've asked her to sit in today, as her company has an interest in the case."

"What company is that?" he inquired.

"The Second Century Insurance Company. Your sister had several policies with our company."

Harper sat up a little straighter in his chair as he became more interested in the conversation. "How do I get my insurance money?"

Marla Jo glanced over at Donovan. "Detective, should I answer Mr. Harper?"

"Go ahead," Donovan replied.

"First of all, Mr. Harper, the policy that lists you as the beneficiary is with a different company. I doubt that the company will release any money until your sister's murder is solved. Right now, we are still investigating her death and it looks like it could be some time before any insurance claims will be paid. I know that our company will not be paying out until the case is closed. I'm sure the other companies have the same policy."

"Well, I sure as hell didn't kill her, so I don't see why I should have to wait."

"If your sister knew she was ill before she applied for those policies, those policies will not be paid," Donovan told him.

"Hold on, Detective. I've paid a fortune in premiums the past four years and now you're telling me I may not get my money?" Harper asked, raising his voice.

"As I said, if Barbara knew she was ill and didn't declare it when she initially applied for those policies, it would be considered fraud, and the policies would be void."

"Barbara didn't know she had cancer until 2015. She had those policies already."

"Perhaps. We're checking on that. Now, could you tell me where you were on the day that Barbara was murdered?"

"I was home all day working, just like every other day of my life."

"You work out of your house?" Donovan asked.

"That's right."

"And, just what is it you do, Mr. Harper?"

"I repair computers."

"Is there anyone that can confirm you were there the entire day?" Donovan asked.

Harper sat back and thought for a moment. "Several customers stopped in."

"Could you give me the names of those people and the times they were there?"

Harper sighed. "I don't remember exactly. I believe they were all afternoon appointments, though. Barbara was murdered in the afternoon, right?"

"I'll need you to write down the names, Mr. Harper, so I can check them out."

"Plus," Harper said proudly, "my girlfriend was there for a while. She stopped by for lunch."

"You have a girlfriend?" Marla Jo blurted out, looking surprised.

"Marla Jo!" Donovan exclaimed.

"Sorry," Marla Jo said.

"That's all right, Detective," Harper said. "I'm used to it. Just because I'm short, people are surprised when they hear that I have a girlfriend."

"Sure, that's why," Marla Jo muttered softly under her breath.

"Ms. McKnight, one more outburst from you, and I'll have to ask you to leave the room," Donovan said as he fought to hold back a grin.

"Sorry," Marla Jo said again.

"Mr. Harper, I wish to apologize to you for Ms. McKnight's behavior. Now, if you'll just write down the names of your customers and the name of your lady friend, I'd appreciate it."

"I can go then?" Harper asked.

"Of course," Donovan said.

"One more thing, Detective."

"Yes."

"If there is any question as to my whereabouts when my sister was being attacked, all you have to do is check my phone and my computer."

"We will if it comes to that," Donovan said. "Again, thank you for your cooperation."

Harper looked over at Marla Jo. "You should remember, Ms. McKnight," he said emphasizing the Ms., "that there is someone out there for everyone. Perhaps, one day you'll be lucky enough to find your soulmate, too."

Donovan shook his head agreeing with him. "You're right, Mr. Harper. I, too, believe that there is someone for everyone." He glanced over at Marla Jo. "He's right, you know. I'm sure you'll find someone someday. Just be patient and don't give up," he told her, trying to keep a straight face.

10

"Well, thanks for that," Marla Jo said as Roger Harper exited the interview room.

"Don't you have any control over that mouth of yours?" Donovan asked, grinning.

"I really am sorry, Bobby. It just slipped out."

"I'm not sure I should allow you in the room when I talk to Alex Morris. Perhaps, you should watch from the other room."

"Nooo. Come on, Donovan, I'll keep quiet."

He looked at her, shaking his head. "I don't know if I can. . ."

"Please," she pleaded, interrupting.

Donovan picked his vibrating phone up from off the table and checked his texts. "Morris is here. You promise to behave?"

"I do," Marla Jo replied.

Donovan walked over to the door and opened it. He glanced down the hall where a young man was sitting. "Mr. Morris?" he called out. "Would you like to come in?"

Marla Jo stared at Alex Morris as he entered the room. "Oh, my God," she muttered.

Donovan glanced over at her and shook his head no.

Morris was what most women would call a dreamboat. Marla Jo could not take her eyes off of him. He was tall, dark, and handsome. Actually, Marla Jo thought, he is positively gorgeous. As Morris glanced over at her and smiled, she suddenly felt warm all over.

"Ma'am," he said, acknowledging her.

"Mr. Morris, this is Marla Jo McKnight. I've asked her to join us today. Her company is investigating the legality of some of the insurance policies that Mrs. Stiverson had with the company she works with."

"Nice," Morris said, looking Marla Jo over.

"You have a beautiful tan," Marla Jo commented.

"Thank you, ma'am."

"Do you object to her being here?" Donovan asked him, as he glared at Marla Jo.

"Heck, no. It's real nice to meet you."

"You, too," Marla Jo stammered.

Donovan looked at her and frowned. "Are you okay, Ms. McKnight.? Can I get you something to drink?"

Marla Jo smiled and shook her head no. "I'm fine, thanks."

Donovan turned to Morris. "How about you? Can I get you something?"

"I'm good. Is this going to take long?"

"It shouldn't. I have a couple of questions for you and once you've answered them, you can be on your way."

"Shoot."

"I would like to know where you were when Mrs. Stiverson was murdered."

"I'm not sure," Morris replied.

"Really?" Donovan said, looking surprised. "And, why would that be?"

"Because I don't know when she was murdered exactly. Nobody has told me anything. I figure it had to be after I left the house, but I'm not sure when it happened. How can I tell you where I was if I don't know what time she was killed?"

"How about you walk us through your day?" Donovan asked.

"The whole day? Well, let me see. I got up around

five, like I usually do, and went for a run. Then, I showered and went for a swim. Mary came out to the pool around eight and told me that Barbara was awake, so I got dressed and went inside so we could do her exercises."

"That would be Mary Johanson?" Donovan asked.

"Right."

Marla Jo wrote something on a piece of paper and slid it over to Donovan. He glanced at it and turned it over.

"Did you live in Mrs. Stiverson's house?"

"Oh, no. I lived in the guest house in the back of the house."

"How long did you live there?" Donovan inquired.

"I moved in about six months after I started taking care of Barbara. She thought it would be more convenient if I was close by and - hey – who wouldn't want to live on a beautiful estate like hers?"

"So, how long ago was that?" Donovan asked.

Morris thought for a moment. "It was 2014. In the spring. Man, it's been five years. That time has sure flown by."

"How was she feeling on the day that she died? I mean, was she in good spirits, feeling okay, or what. You said she did exercises. What kind of exercises?"

"Oh, nothing strenuous. Just mostly exercising her arm and leg muscles. If I recall correctly, we cut it short that day because she wasn't feeling well. Of course, the cancer was getting worse every day. I tell you, Detective, I don't know how she hung on for all those years. She was a pretty tough lady, but you could tell that the fight had pretty much gone."

"What about the rest of the day?"

"I was off the rest of the day. I met up with a few friends and we went to the beach. I thought Mary would be there in case Barbara needed anything. I heard that Mary thought I was in the guest house when she decided to go shopping. Total mix-up on our part."

"So, Barbara was alone in the house after what time would you say?"

"I left around eleven and Mary said she left to go shopping around one or one-thirty."

"I'd like you to write down the names of your friends that went with you to the beach."

"Be glad to," Morris told him. "You gonna check me out?"

"You can be sure of it," Donovan said.

Marla Jo slid another piece of paper toward Donovan. He read it and nodded. "You're paying the premiums on a $250,000.00 policy. Those premiums are kind of steep, Morris. How can you afford it?"

Alex Morris grinned. "Barbara was a very generous person and she paid well. I lived there rent-free, ate whatever I wanted, didn't pay any utilities, and I had the use of any one of her cars. I've saved a lot of money in the past five years, Detective. Paying those premiums was a drop in the bucket considering the money I made."

"So, you're no longer living on the premises?"

Morris shrugged his shoulders. "Nope. I was asked to leave right after she was murdered."

"So, where are you living now?" Donovan asked him.

"I'm staying with a friend. I plan on buying me a nice little condo with the insurance money I'll be getting."

Donovan sighed as Marla Jo passed him another piece of paper. He glanced down at it. "Did Mrs. Stiverson know she had cancer when you started working for her in the spring of 2014?"

Morris looked confused. "I'm not sure. She knew she was sick, but. . ."

"She must have told you something."

"I can't remember," Morris said.

"Well, when did you find out she had cancer?"

Morris looked over at the door. "Are we about done? I'd like to leave now."

"You can leave as soon as you answer that question. When did you find out she had cancer?"

"I'm not sure, man. All these dates are confusing me."

"Take a guess," Donovan prompted.

"I guess it was a few months after I started working there. Yeah, that's right. I asked her about some of the drugs she was taking. So, it had to be then. I guess it was around the 4th of July."

"Excuse me, Detective. I was wondering if I could ask Mr. Morris a question."

Donovan hesitated. "Is it pertinent to the case?"

"It is."

"Go ahead."

"Mr. Morris, I just want to be sure I have the dates correct. You started working for Mrs. Stiverson in 2014. Is that correct?"

"Sure is," Morris told her.

"And, shortly after you started working for her, Mrs. Stiverson told you that she had been battling cancer since 2012. Right?"

"Yes, Ma'am."

"Do you know who else knew this?"

"I figure everyone that she was close to did."

"And, in 2015, Mrs. Stiverson took out a life

insurance policy for $250,000, naming you beneficiary, and you have been paying the premiums for this policy. Do I have all of this right?"

Morris smiled. "You sure do. That's how it happened."

"Thank you, Mr. Morris." Marla Jo put her hand on Donovan's shoulder. "Excuse me, Detective. I'll be back in a moment." She got up from the table and walked out of the room. She walked down to the end of the hall, entered a restroom, threw her arms up in the air, and yelled, "Yes! Yes! Yes! We gotcha, you dumb ass sucker."

She glanced in the mirror, walked out of the room and back down the hall to the interview room, walked in, and sat down.

Donovan gave her a puzzling look. "Is everything okay?"

Marla Jo grinned. "Everything is great."

11

Marla Jo sat back and watched as Alex Morris finished writing the list with the names of the people he went to the beach with. He slid the legal pad across the table to Donovan. "Can I go now?" he asked.

"Just one more thing, if you don't mind," Donovan replied. "This conversation has been recorded and I would like you to confirm that everything you have told me here today is the truth."

"No problem. I've never been one for lying. I figure if you don't lie you don't have to worry trying to remember what you said."

"That's an excellent policy. You can either write it down or speak into the recorder. Your choice."

"Should I just talk normal like?" Morris asked.

"Right. Just talk into this recorder."

"I think I'd rather write it down," Morris told him, changing his mind.

"That's fine. I'll leave you to it," Donovan said, pushing the pad of paper across the table. "I'll be right around the corner at my desk. You can bring it out to me when you're done." Donovan headed for the door, expecting Marla Jo to follow him. When he realized she wasn't behind him, he turned and looked at her. "M. J.?"

"Yes?" she answered, staring at Alex Morris.

"We're done here. Would you like to leave the room?"

"Not really," she said, still staring at the young man.

"Ms. McKnight, would you come with me, please?" Donovan asked, starting to get irritated by her behavior.

Marla Jo looked up at him and grinned. "Do I have to?"

Donovan took a deep breath and let it out. "Yes, you have to."

"Bye, Alex," she said. "It was nice meeting you."

Morris glanced up at her and smiled. "Pleasure was all mine, ma'am."

Marla Jo reached into her purse and took out her phone. "I was wondering if you would mind if I took your picture before I leave."

"Ma'am?"

"Would you stand up for a second so I can take your picture?"

As Morris started to stand up, Donovan walked back into the room and took Marla Jo's arm. "That's enough. Let's go."

Marla Jo raised her phone and snapped a picture of Morris. "Got it. Thanks," she said, as she put her phone back into her purse.

"What the hell do you think you're doing?" Donovan whispered as he ushered her out of the interview room and into the hallway.

"Nothing," Marla Jo said, grinning. "I wanted a picture of the person who just saved my company a small fortune."

"Yeah, that's what you wanted."

"God, Donovan. Isn't he the most beautiful specimen of a man that you've ever seen? He's perfect."

"And, dumb as a box of rocks."

"You think?" she asked.

"Is that what you go for, M. J.? I never pictured you getting all hot and bothered over a kid like that."

Marla Jo laughed. "I swear you sound a little jealous, Detective Bobby Donovan."

"Me? Jealous? You're kidding, right? It's time to get

over yourself, M. J. You couldn't be more wrong," he told her, starting to sound upset.

"Whoa. Don't get mad. I'm sorry. I was only joking, Bobby."

"You have a really weird sense of humor."

"Seriously, I just wanted to see if I'd get a reaction from you, that's all."

"That's what you wanted? Well, how do you like this reaction?" Donovan pushed the door to the restroom open, grabbed Marla Jo, and shoved her into the room.

"What do you. . ."

He pulled her close to him, leaned down, and kissed her.

She only hesitated for a second before she wrapped her arms around his neck and returned his kiss.

Donovan pulled back and gazed into her eyes. "Wow!"

Marla Jo grinned. "Wow is right," she agreed, as she pulled him close to her and kissed him again.

Marla Jo was surprised to see an elderly white-haired woman sitting behind the receptionist's desk.

The woman looked up and smiled. "May I help you?" you asked sweetly.

"I'm Ms. McKnight and you are?"

"Oh, my, it's so nice to meet you, Ms. McKnight. I'm Ida. Ida Itzie, your temporary secretary. The agency sent me over."

"Welcome aboard, Ida. Did you say your last name is Itzie?" she asked, trying not to smile."

"Yes, ma'am."

"Interesting name. But, please, Ida, call me Marla Jo."

"Fine. I will," Ida replied.

"Have you familiarized yourself with everything?"

"Oh, my, yes. I've used all these machines before."

"Machines?"

"You know. Copy machines, computer machines, phones with all kinds of different lines – I've used them all."

"That's good to know," Marla Jo told her as she walked towards her office. "If you need anything, just ask."

"Fine. Can I bring you a cup of coffee?"

Marla Jo smiled. "That sounds good. I could use an eye-opener right about now."

"Yes, Ida?" Marla Jo asked as her intercom buzzed again. "What is it now?"

"There's a man named Brownie on the phone for you. Should I put him through?"

"Please." Marla Jo waited for a second and then hit a button on her phone. "Brownie, how are you?"

"I'm fine. I'm glad I caught you in."

"It's only four o'clock here."

"Right. It's ten here, you know."

Marla Jo smiled. "I know. Why are you working so late?"

"Not working. I'm at home, but I wanted to give you a call before I retired for the evening. I have some news for you."

"Good news, I hope."

"I think you will be more than pleased. The lady you asked me to check on. . ." He hesitated.

"Barbara Stiverson," Marla Jo prompted.

"Right. Stiverson. Anyway, my dear, she saw a Dr.

Floyd Ridman back in 2012. I talked to him and he was distressed to find out that Mrs. Stiverson had been murdered. He said that she probably would have been dead in a month or so anyway."

"He remembered her from seven years ago?"

"He remembered her from seven weeks ago. She was still seeing him."

"What? What do you mean?"

"He was treating her for her cancer. At first, she would fly to London for her treatments, but when she reached the point of being too sick to travel, he came to her."

"I can't believe it. That must have cost her a fortune," Marla exclaimed.

"Believe me, he was well paid. I imagine an examination of her financials will show the dates of travel and the amounts she paid him."

"Brownie, is there any chance that we can get copies of her records?"

"That doesn't seem to be a problem with Dr. Ridman. He told me that he would be glad to give me copies to send to you. He said that as long as she was dead, all doctor/patient confidentiality was null and void.
"

"Brownie, if you were here right now, I'd plant a big wet one right on your mouth. Do you realize how much money you have helped save this company?"

"I gather it's a lot. A big wet one, huh?"

"It's over two million, Brownie. That's big."

"Darn you, Marla Jo. Now all I can think of is that kiss."

"You'll send me the information, right?"

"As soon as I get it from the good doctor," Brownie

replied.

"I owe you a dinner at the finest restaurant in town. No, a car. I owe a car. Seriously, I owe you big time for this, Brownie. Any chance you'll be coming to the States soon?"

"I wish there was, but alas, my work keeps me here for now."

"I miss you," Marla Jo told him.

"And, I miss you and your family. How is everyone?"

"Dad died last Sunday, Brownie. It was fast and we still don't know what happened."

"I'm sorry to hear that, Marla Jo."

"Well, at least mom doesn't have to put up with his crap anymore."

"She did put up with a lot, bless her soul. It was probably his heart or maybe his liver couldn't take any more booze."

"He was such a good man before he started drinking."

"I know, Marla Jo. But, sometimes that devil water can ruin a good man. I guess that's what happened with your dad. I'll say a prayer for him and your mama."

"Thanks, Brownie. Take care of yourself."

"I will, girl. And, Marla Jo?"

"Yes?"

"I'll say a prayer for you, too."

"I appreciate that, Brownie. I can use all the help I can get."

12

Marla Jo grabbed her purse, turned out the light, and walked into the reception area. "Ida, go home. It's after five."

"Could you hold one moment? Thank you." Ida hit the hold button on her phone and looked at Marla Jo. "There's a call for you. Do you want me to take a message?"

"Who is it?"

"A detective. . ." she hesitated. "I don't think he said his last name."

"Detective Donovan?" Marla Jo asked her.

Ida smiled. "That's it. Do you want to talk to him?"

"I'll take it in my office," Marla Jo said. "Now you go on home and I'll see you tomorrow."

Ida picked up the phone. "She'll be with you in just a moment, sir," she said.

Marla Jo hurried into her office and picked up the phone. "Bobby, you just caught me. What's up?"

"I wondered if you're busy tonight."

"Sorry, but I'm on my way to my mom's house."

"Of course. I imagine there's a lot to take care of. When is the funeral?"

"Day after tomorrow. However, mom has pretty much taken care of all the plans and there's not much left to do. Maybe I could meet you later for a drink."

Donovan didn't respond.

"Did I lose you, Bobby?"

"Sorry, I have to go. The coroner is on the phone. I'll call you later."

Marla Jo stared at the phone, realizing that

Donovan had hung up, and shrugged. "That's the second or third time he's done that," she mumbled. "I'm getting a little tired of it."

"Good morning. How may I help you?"

"Ida, it's Marla Jo."

"Good morning, Ms. McKnight. How are you doing this morning?"

"I'm fine. I'll need you to hold down the fort today and tomorrow."

"You won't be in?"

"We've got the wake today and the funeral tomorrow."

"I'm so sorry about your dad. I just found out about it this morning. Is there anything I can do for you?"

"Thanks. No, not really. Just take care of the office for me," Marla Jo said.

"I'll be happy to. Now you take care of yourself and, again, I'm so sorry for your loss."

"And, Ida?"

"Yes?"

"I'm expecting a fax from London. When it comes in, please be sure you put it in the middle top drawer of my desk. It's extremely important."

"Should I call you when it arrives?"

"Just send me a text. But, be sure you put it in my desk. Okay?"

"Got it. Bye now."

"What time does the wake start?" Donovan asked Marla Jo as she sat down at the table.

"Six o'clock. It's between six and eight." She sighed. "I hate this."

"I know. It's rough."

"This is a nice break though," she said, smiling.

"I'm sorry about yesterday. I didn't mean to cut you off like that, but I had to take that phone call."

"No problem," Marla Jo replied. "Thanks for asking me to lunch. Mother and grandma were driving me crazy."

"I figured you could use a break. Besides, I wanted to let you know that I've got the coroner's report on Barbara Stiverson."

"That took long enough," Marla Jo commented.

"It's hard to autopsy a body when you don't have all the pieces."

"I guess. So, what killed her? Stabbed, strangled, or shot?"

Donovan grinned. "Nope. None of the three. He says she was injected with a huge amount of potassium chloride. It's almost impossible to detect in a body but, fortunately, he found traces of it."

"I hope she was dead before she was cut up."

"Looks like it, from the amount of blood we found. There would have been more if she had been alive."

"Well, that's a blessing. I'd hate to think she was still alive while being chopped to pieces. Did you guys ever find her arm and the other stuff that was missing?"

"Nope. Whoever killed her took it all with them." Donovan hesitated a few seconds. "Plus a few toes," he blurted out.

"Toes? Someone cut off her toes?"

"Just a few. The little piggies were missing."

That's so sick," Marla Jo exclaimed.

"The doc didn't notice it right away, with all the parts being in different bags and all. But, sure enough, those two toes are gone."

Marla Jo took a bite of her sandwich. 'I just don't understand how people can do such things."

"It takes all kinds," Donovan commented. "FYI, I talked to Richard Stiverson and David Freemont. I have some doubts about Stiverson. He says he was fishing at Sunset Lake and, although I have a witness who saw his car there, the witness wasn't sure who was driving it. He thought it was a much younger man, but he didn't get a good look at the person."

"What about her son?" Marla Jo asked.

"That's a tough one. He says he was home sick and in bed most of the day. Right now, I've got nothing to go on, except his word."

"Maybe he saw a doctor. Have you checked that out?"

"In process."

Marla Jo sat back and thought. "What if he drove Stiverson's car to Sunset Lake while Stiverson was cutting up Barbara?"

Donovan grinned. "God, you have such an imagination."

"No, Bobby. It's possible."

"And, who killed Barbara? Neither one of them was at her house that morning."

"Morris was. I would think he would be your likely suspect, being her healthcare provider and all. He killed her and then went to the beach with his friends. Her son, David, then drove Stiverson's car to the lake while Stiverson cut her up." Marla Jo sat back in her chair and smiled. "There. Case solved."

"One question," Donovan said.

"What?"

"Why bother to cut Stiverson up? Why not inject her with the potassium chloride and let everyone think she died of natural causes? She was sick and she was dying."

"That's easy," Marla Jo told him. "To cover up the way she was murdered. To make it look like a break-in. Hell, how do I know? It's your case, Bobby. You solve it. I've already got what I need from this case," she told him, grinning.

Donovan stared at her. "You talked to your friend in London, didn't you?"

"I sure did. Barbara Stiverson knew in 2012 that she had cancer. All the policies that were taken out after that date are void. Right now, the only people who benefit from her death are Richard Stiverson and her kids. And, the small amount she left the church in her Will, of course."

"I'll be damned. You lucked out."

"And. . ." Marla Jo smiled, looking pleased with herself. "And, if Richard Stiverson killed or had her killed, he doesn't get a penny. So, please prove he killed her, will you?"

Donovan sat back in his chair, shaking his head. "You're sure of this? I mean, about the policies."

"Absolutely. Every policy written after 2012 is being kicked to the curb. That's over two million dollars, Bobby, for just my company. And, almost two million for the other insurance companies."

"That's a lot of money, M. J.," he stated.

"It is. And, Stiverson is set to get a million five-plus unless – well, you know."

"Well, you may be paying him because right now we have diddly squat to prove he did anything wrong."

"You want a refill or do you need to get going?" Marla Jo asked, motioning to his coffee cup.

"Yeah, I could use a little more." He held up his cup and motioned to the waitress. "She's coming," he told Marla Jo. "There's one more thing I need to discuss with you before I leave."

"What's that?" Marla Jo asked.

"I got the autopsy report on your dad, M. J."

Marla Jo stared at him. "And?" she asked.

"I'm afraid it's not good news."

"Why is that?"

"Your dad didn't die from natural causes."

13

"No way," Marla Jo cried out, looking totally shocked. "There is no way anyone in my family killed my dad. You're wrong, Donovan."

"I wish I was, but the coroner found traces of poison in his system."

"Have him check it again," she pleaded, trying to hold back the tears. "He made a mistake. I know he did."

Donovan reached across the table and took her hand. "He didn't make a mistake. I'm sorry."

Marla Jo dabbed at her eyes with her napkin. "How?"

Donovan looked confused. "How what?"

"How did it happen? We all ate and drank the same things. What could he have ingested that the rest of us didn't? Why aren't we all dead?" She sat back and stared at Donovan.

"I can't tell you. . ."

"Of course, you can't," Marla Jo interrupted. "Because the coroner made a mistake."

"Here's what I can tell you," Donovan said. "It had to have been added to something he ate by someone in the kitchen."

"But, he served himself from the table." She thought for a moment. "Except for. . ." She looked at Donovan and shook her head no.

"Except for the pudding," Donovan said, completing her sentence.

"There is no way grandma would have poisoned him, Bobby."

"She put poop in his pudding. She may have added

a little poison while she was at it."

"Wait a minute," Marla Jo cried out. "The wine."

"What about it?"

"He was the only one that drank any of the wine."

"We all drank some wine," Donovan said, looking slightly confused.

"Not from the last bottle. The one that Pete got from the kitchen when he went to get Dad's presents. Remember? Dad spilled it all over everything."

Donovan closed his eyes and let out a big sigh, upset that he had forgotten about the wine. "Shit!" he exclaimed, causing the people at the table next to him to look over at him. "Sorry," he told them.

"So, maybe it wasn't the pudding after all," Marla Jo declared.

"Do you remember if the bottle was open when Pete brought it in from the kitchen?" Donovan asked her.

Marla Jo closed her eyes, trying to remember. "It was open," she finally told him.

"Are you sure?"

"I'm 99% sure," she replied.

"Shit," Donovan whispered. "That means that anyone who was in the kitchen could have opened that bottle and put poison in it."

"I don't think grandma could have opened it. Her hands aren't strong enough to pull a cork out of a bottle."

"Are you sure the bottle was corked or was it a screw-on cap?"

"Hell, I don't know, Bobby. I'm just thinking out loud here. You bagged everything. Check it out."

Donovan shook his head no. "I don't think we have the wine bottle."

"Seriously?" Marla Jo said, looking shocked.

"I don't remember seeing it."

"Nice work, Detective." Marla Jo smiled.

"Don't rub it in."

"The bottle is gone, the mess has been cleaned up, and the glass he drank from has been washed. So, if the poison was in the wine, there is no way to prove it. Or, who might have put it there."

Donovan sat back in his chair and frowned. "Who took the wine bottle?" he mused. "It was on the table when your dad died. If it had been there when my men were gathering evidence we would have it. Someone must have taken it before my guys got there."

"I don't know and I think it's a moot point anyway," Marla Jo said. "No one put poison in the wine."

"It could have been in the pudding, you know," Donovan stated.

"And, that you can check out, seeing as how the rest of the pudding was bagged by your men. So, please check it out and let me know what you find. But, right now, I have to move my butt and go home and change." Marla Jo stood up and smiled. "Thanks for lunch."

"Wait a minute. I'll walk you out," Donovan said as he reached for his wallet.

"Can I leave the tip?"

"I've got it," he told her as he threw a couple of bills on the table.

"Next time I'll treat."

"We'll see," he replied as he followed her to the exit and pushed the door open. Donovan took her hand and pulled her in close. "I'll call you," he said as he bent down and gently kissed her. "God, you are really short," he joked.

"I am not. You're just extremely tall," Marla Jo

replied. "And, good looking," she added. She turned and walked towards her car. "See ya."

Donovan watched her as she walked away, wondering just what the hell he was doing. "This could be the biggest mistake of my life," he muttered under his breath.

At eight o'clock, the funeral director closed the doors to the room where Frank McKnight was laid out. Marla Jo looked at her family, who were sitting and talking to each other, and wondered if they felt like the whole thing had been a waste of time.

"How many people signed the book?" Betsy asked Suzie.

"I counted fifteen, but a few people didn't sign it."

"That's not a very big turnout, is it?" Charlotte commented.

"I figure there will be even less for the funeral tomorrow," Pete said.

"Let's face it. Dad wasn't liked by very many people," Marla Jo declared. "I only saw two of his old drinking buddies here to pay their respect. The rest of the people were friends of mom."

"I'm thinking about calling off the luncheon. It doesn't make a lot of sense to go to all that trouble and expense for a handful of people," Betsy said. "What do you think, Pete?"

"I think we should still do it. Who knows who may show up tomorrow."

"I guess," Betsy said. "Well, I'm tired. I'm going home."

"Before we all leave, there's something I need to tell you all," Marla Jo told them. "I had lunch with Detective

Donovan today."

"I heard," Suzie said. "What's up with you two anyway?"

"Nothing is up, Suzie. Donovan told me that he got the autopsy report – the final one."

"We knew that already," Pete said. "They wouldn't have released the body if the results weren't completed."

"There's more, Pete. They found poison in his system. Dad was poisoned by something. Right now, they are considering this a murder."

"Oh, dear Lord, no," Betsy cried out. "I can't believe it. Who would do such a thing?"

"Well, it doesn't surprise me," Charlotte said. "Everyone sitting here had a reason to want him dead. So, tell me which one of you did the family the favor? I'd like to shake your hand."

"Mother! That's a horrible thing to say," Betsy said.

"It's true and you know it," Charlotte declared. "So, Marlie, who does the good detective suspect?"

"Grandma, I haven't a clue. All I know, for sure, is that as soon as the funeral is over tomorrow every one of you will be questioned. The only reason you aren't all sitting in a room down at the police station right now is because Detective Donovan is doing me a favor. So, heads up, you all, because the next few days are going to be rough."

"Damn," Charlotte suddenly cried out. "He thinks it was me, doesn't he? He thinks I poisoned the pudding."

"Well, you did put dog shit in it, Grandma," Suzie said. "I would suspect you, too."

"Suzie! That's enough," Betsy yelled. She looked over at Marla Jo. "What do you think we should do?"

Marla Jo shrugged. "Just cooperate with him. The

police lab is still checking the food they bagged, but they will probably have the final results by tomorrow sometime. If they don't find what the poison was in. . ." She sighed. "Maybe, that is a good thing. I don't know what to tell you. Just be honest with him."

"What else, Marlie?" Betsy asked.

"What do you mean?" Marla Jo replied, looking confused.

"You're holding back something. I can always tell when you are hiding something."

"I'm tired, Mom. Just like you and everyone else. So, how about we all get out of here and get some rest? Grandma, do you need a ride home?"

"Thanks, but Suzie and Mark are dropping me off."

"All right. I'm out of here," Marla Jo declared as she stood up. "I'll see you all tomorrow."

"Marla Jo?" Charlotte called out.

Marla Jo turned and looked at her grandmother. "Yes?"

"Maybe, if you're free one day next weekend, you can come over and I'll teach you how to make my bread pudding."

Marla Jo stared at her grandmother, trying to decide if the old woman was serious or trying to be funny.

14

"Is this necessary?" Pete asked. "We just buried my father, for God's sake. It seems to me that you could give us a little time to grieve."

Donovan gave him a disgusted look. "Quit your bellyaching, will you? I should have pulled all of you in for questioning two days ago. And, as far as you grieving, Pete. . . Well, let's just say that I haven't seen any of you do any actual grieving since your father hit the floor a week ago. So, go sit down with the rest of your family."

"I'm leaving and I don't think there's anything you can do to stop me."

"It's either here or down at the station."

Pete started walking to the front door. "I'm out of here."

Donovan glanced over at a uniformed cop who was standing near the door. "Officer Chesterton, would you please help Pete to a chair in the living room?"

Chesterton took two steps towards Pete who held up his arms in surrender. "Okay," he exclaimed. "I'm going."

Donovan followed him into the living room and watched as he made himself comfortable. He looked at the six people and sighed. Next to informing people that a loved one was dead, questioning people that he knew was definitely a part of the job that he truly detested. You wanted to believe that they weren't capable of such an act, yet you had to put your personal feeling aside and do due diligence.

"If you were in the kitchen at any time on the day of Frank's birthday, please raise your hand," he said. Everyone but Mark raised their hand. "All right. Good.

Now, if anyone saw Mark in the kitchen that day, raise your hand."

No one raised their hand.

"Donovan," Marla Jo said.

"Yes."

"Mark never got off of the couch before we sat down for dinner. He never gets off the couch when he's here and he certainly would never go in the kitchen."

"Thank you, Marla Jo," Donovan said.

"You're welcome," she replied, smiling.

"If anyone brought any food or liquor into the house with them on that day, please raise your hand," Donovan asked.

Charlotte's hand shot up immediately.

"Anyone else?" Donovan asked.

"I did," Pete told him.

Everyone in the room stared at him. "What did you bring?" Suzie asked her brother.

"I brought a bottle of wine. You know - the wine we had with dinner."

"That's right," Betsy agreed. "We all had some. Remember, Detective? He opened it right there in the dining room and poured us all a glass."

"Is that the only bottle you brought with you?" Donovan inquired.

"It is," Pete said.

"Can anyone tell me where the bottle of wine, which was in the kitchen while we were eating, came from?" He watched as the six adults shook their heads or shrugged, indicating that none of them knew where it came from.

"None of you know? Betsy, you must have some idea how it got there, don't you?"

"Maybe Frank bought it. He had gone to the liquor

store for some beer earlier in the day." She looked at Donovan and frowned. "I don't know what to tell you."

"I didn't kill him?" Charlotte asked. "I knew it! It was the wine, wasn't it? I knew it wasn't me. I never heard of anyone who died from eating dog poo." She grinned. "Maybe he poisoned himself."

"Anyone else?" Donovan asked ignoring Charlotte. "All right then. We have two people," he said when no one else spoke up.

"Well, actually. . ." Suzie hesitated.

"What? Actually, what?" Mark asked.

"I think the boys may have brought some treats with them,"

Mark looked at her like she was crazy. "Are you saying you think one of our kids brought poison into this house and killed their grandfather? What in the world is wrong with you?"

"I'm not saying that, Mark. But, the detective wants to know and I told him."

"I doubt it was the boys, Mark. Thank you for letting me know that, Suzie," Donovan said. "Now, people, this is what we know so far," he told them, getting their attention. "The wine was most likely poisoned. It was the only thing Frank ingested at the table that none of us had. We know it wasn't the pudding so no worries there, Charlotte. However, every one of you here, except Mark, had access to that wine bottle, so I can't rule any of you out."

"And, me," Marla Jo declared, smiling. "You can rule me out, too."

"Sorry," Donovan said. "I can't rule you out. You were in the kitchen."

"But, you know. . ."

"I'll get back to you," he said interrupting her. "Pete, the wine bottle was open when you brought it to the table. Did you open it in the kitchen before you brought it to the dining room?"

"No, I didn't," Pete declared. "It was already open."

"I see." Donovan thought for a moment. "Well, then I guess the five of you are all suspects at this point."

"Are you sure the wine was poisoned," Marla Jo asked him.

"We assume so," Donovan said.

"Well, did you check out the bottle or the glass he drank from?"

Donovan gave her a dirty look. "As M. J. already knows, they weren't included in the items that we took from the house. By the time we figured out the poison was most likely in the wine, the bottle had been discarded. I'm sorry but it was an unfortunate oversight."

Betsy stared at him. "What the hell, Detective? You don't know what killed him or where it came from, do you? This is all a guessing game on your part." She turned and looked at Marla Jo. "What is going on, Marlie?"

Marla Jo shrugged. "It's the only answer, Mother. It has to have been in the wine."

Mark stood up and brushed off his pants. "Come on, Suzie, let's go. This has been a total waste of time."

"Hold up," Donovan shouted. "There's no doubt in my mind that one of you killed Frank. It's only a matter of time before I find out who it was. It's taken longer than I thought, but the sample we took from the carpet is being tested. We also have men going through the garbage dump looking for the wine bottle and they are good at what they do. I'm giving you a chance right now to fess up before this goes any further." He glanced over at each one of them, waiting for someone to speak up.

Mark looked at Donovan and shook his head. "Unfucking real." He took Suzie's hand, walked to the front door, opened it, and walked out.

Pete looked at Charlotte and smiled. "Want a ride home, Grandma?"

Betsy watched her mother and son walk out of the house. She sat back in her chair and sighed. "Marla Jo, are you sure you want to keep dating this man?" she asked. "He doesn't seem to be very good at what he does."

Marla Jo looked up at Donovan and grinned. "No, I'm not sure, Mom. But, then, I haven't been a party to everything he does yet."

15

Detective Donovan studied the first murder board. He looked at the pictures that he had tacked to the board and reviewed the information regarding the beneficiaries. He still didn't have a clue as to who might have killed Barbara Stiverson and he was getting frustrated. It had been almost two weeks since her body had been found mutilated in her home.

He examined the pictures that had been taken of the different rooms where her body parts had been found. It just didn't make sense why someone would do this to an elderly sick woman who had no way to fight back or protect herself. And, on top of that, what kind of a sicko takes body parts as souvenirs, Donovan asked himself.

The CSI Unit had finished gathering evidence and the house had been released to Barbara Stiverson's family. Bella Francis, Barbara's daughter, had made arrangements for crime scene cleaners to remove any sign of what had happened and any biohazards that resulted from it.

Donovan took a few steps back and turned to look at a second murder board. The case itself, if not as violent, was just as perplexing as the Stiverson case. The very idea that the man had been murdered right in front of him was driving him crazy. Then, to top it off, his men overlooked bagging the wine glass. Plus, he entirely missed the fact that the wine bottle was missing. In all his years on the force, he couldn't remember making such a horrible mistake and he was kicking his ass around the block every time he thought about it.

He was too close to this one. He knew it and he knew

he should step aside and let a different detective take over this case. He also knew he wasn't going to turn it over to anyone. He wanted this one big time.

He stepped back and sat down at his desk, glanced at his watch, and decided it wasn't too late to call M. J. He wanted to hear her voice or maybe ask her out for a drink. "Damn," he uttered. She was getting under his skin and he knew he should back off. At least until this case was closed. He picked up his phone to call her.

"Again, Marla Jo, I'm so sorry," Ida said. "Is it okay if I leave now?"

Marla Jo looked over at the doorway where Ida was standing, holding her coat and purse. "That's fine. I'm about done here. I won't need you for anything else today."

"I just don't know how I could have been so stupid," Ida told her, tears welling up in her eyes.

"Mistakes happen," Marla Jo said. "It's not like we couldn't get another copy. Everything is fine, Ida. Forget about it."

"I'll see you tomorrow?"

"Of course," Marla Jo replied. "Have a nice evening." She smiled as Ida left, shutting the door behind her.

It had been embarrassing to call Brownie and ask him to resend the fax. She had already waited over two weeks for him to get the information from Barbara Stiverson's doctor and she figured she had bothered him enough. She picked up the stack of papers that Brownie had faxed her the second time and started to put them in order. Poor woman, she thought. It must be rough to get to be that age and still have to hold down a job to make ends meet. But, even so, shredding the first fax that

Brownie sent her from London was a little much. She jumped as the phone rang.

"Marla Jo McKnight," she answered.

"Hi. It's Donovan. How would you like to meet somewhere for a drink?"

"I don't know. I've got a ton of work that I need to take care of."

"What are you working on?" Donovan asked her.

"Brownie sent me all the medical records from Stiverson's doctor in London. There are a ton of pages and I'm trying to put them in some type of order."

"Is it something I can help you with? I could pick up some carry-out and bring it over to your office."

"I've got a better idea. How about you bring that carry out to my house instead? I think I've had enough of Barbara Stiverson for today."

"Sounds good. What are you in the mood for? Chinese, Mexican, Italian. . ."

Marla Jo laughed. "Surprise me, Bobby. I'll see you in what? An hour?"

"Make it an hour and a half."

"Okay. See you then," she said as she hung up the phone.

Donovan hung up his phone, reached over, and turned off his desk lamp. He turned in his chair and looked at the McKnight murder board again. He stared at Marla Jo's picture and smiled. Yep, no doubt about it. He was in trouble. He looked at the pictures of the rest of her family that were posted on the board, suddenly feeling that something was missing. He stood up and stared at the pictures. "Son of a bitch!" he exclaimed, as he realized what it was. The grandsons, Mark, Jr. and Casey hadn't been added to the board. He hadn't bothered to talk to them after Frank died and he didn't consider them as suspects but they should have been interviewed.

He shook his head, disgusted with himself for another oversight, and left the room. He had dinner to pick up.

Marla Jo took a sip of wine and sighed. "Thanks for dinner, Bobby. I enjoyed it. I'm glad you called."

"It was good, wasn't it?"

"It was. And, I needed to get out of the office. My temp is starting to get on my nerves and it took everything I have not to ream her ass out today."

Donovan grinned. "I thought you said she was a sweet old lady. What did she do?"

"She shredded every page of the fax that Brownie sent me. I swear there were at least a hundred pages."

Donovan laughed. "Why the hell would she do that?"

"It's not funny," Marla Jo said, grinning. "And, how should I know why she did it? She's old. Who knows why old people do what they do? I told her to put the fax in my desk drawer when it came in. And, what does she do? She shreds it. Do you know how embarrassing it was to have to call and ask Brownie to send it again?"

"Fax machines have memory. Why didn't you just reprint it?"

Marla Jo pretended to be surprised. "They do? Gee, if only I would have known that," she said.

Donovan grinned. "Okay, so you know that. Sorry."

"I do. Unfortunately, our fax machine only saves the last fax received and a few more came in after the one from Brownie."

"But, everything turned out okay, didn't it? Cut the old gal some slack. That may be you someday."

Marla Jo gave him a playful punch on his arm and laughed. "Watch your mouth, Donovan."

"Ouch!" he exclaimed, grinning.

"God, you're such a baby," Marla Jo told him.

"How's it stacking up, anyway?" Donovan asked.

"You mean the insurance claims?"

"Right," he answered.

"None of the policies written after 2012 when she found out she had cancer will be paid out. Everyone jumped on the bandwagon once they found out that Stiverson had cancer. It's just so disgusting, Bobby."

"That only leaves Richard Stiverson to collect from his policies," Bobby declared.

"Unless he is the one that killed Barbara. Until you close that case, he gets nothing." She looked over at him. "Can you believe he's called my office over a dozen times asking for his money?"

"I can believe it. I've talked to him several times and he is one of the most impatient men I've ever met."

"Let's talk about something else, shall we?" Marla Jo asked. "I'm tired of talking about work."

"Just one more thing I need to mention, M. J.," Donovan said.

"What's that?"

"I'm going to have to bring your nephews in for a conversation. No one has. . ."

"What the hell, Bobby! Why?" she yelled

"Please, don't go all ballistic on me. It's routine. They were there when your dad died and I need a statement from them for the record. It's not a big deal, so don't take it the wrong way."

Marla Jo stared at him for a second and then looked away. "I get it. I don't like it, but I understand that you need to do it."

"I'm kinda torn here, you know. Sometimes I think it would be better if I handed this case over to a different detective."

"Why would you do that, Bobby?"

"I'm too close to this one. I really like you, M. J. and I'm not sure if I'm doing the right thing by continuing with this case. I've already made a couple of bad mistakes."

"I'm going to ask you to do two things for me," Marla Jo said.

"What?"

"For starters, I'd like you to call me Marlie. You're the only person who calls me M. J. and I don't care for it. Also, I'm asking. . ."

Donovan held up his hand. "Wait a minute. How long have I known you?"

Marla Jo shrugged. "I don't know. A few years, I guess."

"I've known you for over five years and I have always called you M. J. and now – five years later – you tell me you don't like it?"

"It wasn't important before. Now that I'm seeing more of you, I want you to call me Marlie."

Donovan grinned. "Done. What else?"

"Please stay on the case. I know it's difficult and you're afraid of a conflict of interest and all that crap, but my family trusts you to do the best job, Bobby. We're all afraid of the outcome, you know. I mean, after all, someone killed my dad and. . ." She hesitated and took a deep breath. "I hate to say it, but it must have been someone that was there that day. Unless, he killed himself, of course."

"And, done. I'll stay on the case. However, I'm sure you know that your dad didn't poison himself."

"I know. Just wishful thinking, I guess. Thank you, Bobby."

Donovan reached over, picked up the bottle of wine, and started to top off his glass. Suddenly, he put the bottle down and looked at Marla Jo. "I have a better idea," he said, as he stood up and took her hand.

"Really?" she asked, looking surprised.

"I think it's time that you're party to one of the other things I do," he replied as he pulled her up off the couch.

Marla Jo grinned. "Mom will be so happy to know you're good at something."

"And, you know this how?"

"Am I wrong?"

"Good doesn't even begin to describe it," Donovan said laughing, as he gathered her up in his arms and carried her to the bedroom.

16

Donovan looked up at the woman entering the room and smiled. "Ms. Johanson," he said, acknowledging her. He stood and shook her hand. "What brings you here?"

"Please, don't be so formal. Call me Mary."

"Mary it is. Please have a seat."

"I won't keep you long, Detective, but I thought you might be interested in something I noticed since the house has been released."

"I understand that the cleaners finished up. Will you be staying on there?"

"For now. I'm not sure what Mrs. Stiverson's children will be doing with the place. But, I wanted to tell you that I've noticed some things are missing."

Donovan looked surprised. "Really? If I recall, we asked everyone about this after Mrs. Stiverson's death. Everyone agreed that nothing was missing. So, just what exactly has been taken?"

Mary reached into her purse and took out a piece of folded paper. She unfolded it and handed it to Donovan.

Donovan read through it and smiled. "I don't get it, Mary. This looks like a shopping list."

"Exactly. But, it's not. It's a list of the items that have disappeared from the kitchen."

Donovan shook his head. "Are you saying that these food items were stolen?"

"Exactly. After poor Barbara was killed you asked us to check to see if anything was missing. Her children and I checked everything of value and nothing had been taken as far as we could tell. However, Detective Donovan, I certainly didn't check the kitchen pantry or the freezer. I mean, like, who would? It's not like people are murdered for some canned goods or a pot roast, are they?"

Donovan shook his head no. "Are you sure that Alex Morris didn't take them?

"Mr. Morris hasn't been back on the property since right after Barbara was killed. Bella and David paid him what he was owed plus a nice bonus and asked him to leave. I certainly didn't take any of those items. I stayed with my daughter while the house was being cleaned. Someone took those items, Detective, and unless it was one of your men, it happened when that poor woman was killed. And, then, to be butchered like that. It was a horrible horrible thing that happened to her," she said, wiping a tear away from her eye.

"You're right, it was," Donovan replied, agreeing with her.

Mary leaned closer to him and whispered, "Who do you think did it? You can tell me. I won't say anything."

"We don't know for sure yet," he whispered back. "Who do you think it was?"

"Mary looked around the room, making sure no one was listening. She leaned in closer to Donovan. "My guess is Mr. Stiverson. He has a lot of money coming. Do you think it could be him?"

Donovan shook his head. "I really can't say. But, I'll definitely let you know when we find out. Is there anything else, Mary?" he said quietly.

She thought for a moment. "I guess not. I just thought you should know about this."

"I appreciate it. This has been a big help to us."

"Really? Mary said smiling. "I'm so glad. Are you sure you can't tell me who you think did it?"

Donovan grinned. "Sorry, but no."

"Thanks for your time, sir." Donovan hung up the phone and swore.

"Did you say something?"

"Sorry. Just talking to myself," Donovan told the detective sitting at the desk next to his.

"First sign you're getting old," the detective stated, grinning.

"You think?" Donovan replied. He looked at the notes he had made while talking to Edgar Funk, the principal of the school that the McKnight boys attended. Sighing, he stood up and headed for the door.

"Where you going?" the detective asked.

"To school," Donovan told him, grinning.

"Good. It's about time you got some smarts."

"That's about it," Principal Funk told Donovan, as he closed the manila file in front of him. "As you can see, both of them are basically good students."

Donovan looked at the copies of the boy's report cards. "Good grades." He looked up at Funk. "Have you had any trouble with them?"

"Not at all. They are both quite active in sports and from what their teachers have told me, they enjoy having them in their classes."

Donovan continued to look over the report cards, checking to see what classes they were taking. "I see that Mark has taken a few science classes, such as biology, chemistry, and physics."

"Some of those classes are required," Funk stated.

"Is it possible for me to talk to his biology teacher?"

"I do believe she's in the middle of a class right now,"

Funk replied.

"I only have one fast question for her," Donovan said. "I'd appreciate it if you could point me to her room. I'll only take a minute of her time and I'll be out of everyone's hair. It's so much easier than having to take her to the station to question her."

"Of course, it is," Funk told him. "The biology teacher's name is Mrs. Billington."

"Mrs. Billington it is," Donovan said.

Principal Funk hesitated a moment. "Are you sure we can't do this at a different time? I hate to disturb her."

"I'm here now. I won't keep her long."

Well, if you insist," he said reluctantly. "I'll show you the way," he said, getting out of his chair.

Funk opened the door to the biology room and motioned for Mrs. Billington to come to the door. She glanced over at the principal and frowned. "What is it, Mr. Funk? I'm in the middle of a class."

"I need a moment of your time," he told her.

"Can't it wait?"

"Now, please, Mrs. Billington."

She walked over to the door, obviously upset over being interrupted. "What?" she barked at Funk.

"This is Detective Donovan. He would like a word with you," Funk told her, stepping back away from the woman.

Donovan smiled as he shook the woman's hand. Mrs. Billington looked exactly how Donovan thought a teacher should look. She was middle-aged, slightly overweight, had a big bosom, and wore glasses. She also had an air about her that demanded respect.

"It's nice to meet you. I'm extremely sorry to bother

you during your busy time, Mrs. Billington," Donovan told her. "I thought this would be easier than asking you to come to the police station."

Billington turned beet red. "Am I under arrest?"

"No. Absolutely not and I'm sorry if that's the impression I gave you. I have a question I need to ask you."

"Well, spit it out, Detective. I've got to get back in there. You can't leave those kids alone, you know."

"At any time during the school year do you study poisonous plants?"

"That's a strange question, Detective," she replied.

He looked at her, waiting for an answer.

"We study botany if that's what you're asking," she said.

"That's not exactly what I asked, Mrs. Billington. What about poisonous plants? Is that a subject that you study?"

"Detective, we have a lot of children who spend time in the woods. Some hike, some hunt, and some go camping or fishing with their parents. Whatever the situation, I feel it is my duty to inform them of the dangers of wild plants so they know which ones are poisonous. It is always tempting to try a berry or two from some unknown plant." She looked up at him. "Do you understand what I'm saying, Detective Donovan?"

Donovan stared at her. "I think so," he said feeling uncomfortable. "I gather that's a yes, then."

"I believe that's what I said, Detective. If you have any other questions, kindly call and make an appointment. Interrupting a teacher in the middle of a class is extremely rude. Your mother should have taught you as much," Billington stated, as she opened the door and walked back into her classroom.

"You could have given me a heads up," Donovan told Funk.

Funk grinned. "What? And, miss all this? Besides, I hate to admit it, but that woman scares the crap out of me."

17

Donovan glanced at his phone. It was M. J. calling. He hesitated, trying to decide if he should ignore the call or pick up.

"Do you need to get that, Detective?" Suzie Cox asked sarcastically.

Deciding to ignore the call, he glanced at her. "I appreciate that you brought the boys in. I know you have other things you could be doing right now and don't want to be here. However, it's imperative that I talk to Mark, Jr., and Casey. I should have interviewed them right after your dad died but I kind of. . ."

"You kind of what?" Suzie interrupted. "Forgot about it? Is that why you waited until now? Have you run out of people to accuse and now you're picking on my boys?"

"I wanted to check a few things out before I talked to them, Mrs. Cox. So, how about you drop the attitude and let me get on with this?"

Suzie gave him a dirty look and glanced away. She let out a big sigh and sat back in her chair. "I'm sorry I snapped, but this is very troubling to me."

"I understand that, but this isn't a big deal. I need their statements for the record. As soon as I'm done asking them a few questions, you can leave. Okay?"

"I guess," Suzie said.

"Good," Donovan said. He looked across the table at Mark, Jr. "Mark, I'd like you to tell me why you were in your grandma's kitchen that day."

"Wait a minute," Suzie exclaimed. She looked over at Donovan. "Do we need a lawyer here, Detective?"

"Of course not. That's not necessary. I just need to clear up a few things. However, I need to talk to Mark without any interruptions. Okay?"

Suzie shook her head yes.

"Can you answer my question, Mark?"

"Mom?" Mark said, looking at his mother. "Do I have to answer him?"

"Just answer his questions, Mark," Suzie replied.

"Could you tell me what you were doing in the kitchen?" Donovan asked the boy again.

"I don't know," Mark told him.

"Well, you must have gone in there for a reason. Do you remember what it was? Did you want something that was in the kitchen?"

"I guess."

"Can you tell me what it was?" Donovan asked, trying to be patient with Mark.

"Me and Casey wanted some soda," he told Donovan, still looking down at his hands.

"Casey and I," Suzie corrected him.

Donovan glanced at her. "Please, Mrs. Cox."

"Sorry," Suzie said.

"Where's Casey?" Mark suddenly asked.

"Casey and your dad are talking to another detective in the room next door."

"What is that detective asking him?" Mark asked, looking nervous.

"He's probably asking him the same questions I'm asking you, Mark. Why? Does that bother you?" Donovan asked.

"Uh-uh. I was just wondering, is all."

"So, Mark, did you know I talked to your biology teacher the other day?"

"I heard. So what?" Mark said, slouching further down in his chair.

"Mark, will you please sit up straight?" Suzie asked.

Donovan gave her a look.

"Sorry," she said, looking away.

"Have you been in any woods lately?"

"Mom?" Mark whined.

"Maybe we should stop here," Suzie told Donovan. "I think we need an attorney."

Donovan sat back in his chair and stared at Suzie. "Mrs. Cox, would you like to tell me what's going on here? It's kind of obvious that Mark is hiding something and. . ." He turned and looked towards the door as it swung open. "I'm busy here," he said.

"A word, please, Detective."

Donovan stood up and walked to the door. "What is it?"

"In the hall, please."

Donovan stepped into the hall and closed the door behind him. "What is it?" he repeated.

"That Casey kid gave it up," he told Donovan. "His brother poisoned the wine."

"Casey told you that Mark killed his grandfather?" Donovan asked, looking surprised.

"He did. Supposedly, it was an accident. Mark learned about different types of poisonous berries in school. He went exploring in the woods and found some plants he thought looked like the ones in his biology book. He messed around and made some type of a liquid mixture with them."

"Are you kidding me?" Donovan exclaimed.

"Nope. He said his brother thought the berries would only make his grandfather sick. He certainly didn't think it would kill anyone. He just wanted to see his grandfather puke, as he put it. The kid said that his brother has been a nervous wreck ever since it happened."

"The berries were poisonous and he didn't think it would kill him? How stupid is this kid, anyway?"

The detective shrugged. "You tell me. You're the one who is interviewing him. Anyway, that's what the kid told me. His dad is super pissed, let me tell you."

"Ah, shit, man. This is gonna kill his mother," Donovan grumbled.

"Yeah? Well, his father isn't looking too good right now. He's asked for an attorney, so I had to stop questioning the kid."

"All right. You go back in there and keep the old man talking. I'm going to see if I can get Mark, Jr. to fess up and tell me what he did. If I can get a confession out of him before his mother asks for a lawyer, we may get what we need."

"It's worth a try."

Donovan went back into the interview room and sat down across from Mark and his mother. "I just found out what happened, Mark. Casey told us what you did and that it was an accident. We know you didn't mean to do it."

Mark reached for his mother's hand. "I didn't. I didn't mean to do it, Mom. I just thought it would make him a little sick, that's all. I'm so sorry," he told her as he started to cry. "Please, forgive me."

Suzie reached for her son and wrapped her arms around him, holding him tight. "Of course, you didn't mean to hurt grandpa. It was an accident. I understand," she said as the tears rolled down her cheeks.

"I'm going to go get someone from the District Attorney's office and see if we can make a deal here, Mrs. Cox. I'm sure if they know it wasn't intentional, they will work with you. I do need to read Mark his rights first, but it's just a formality."

"Thank you, Detective," Suzie said. She sat back in her chair, tears streaming down her cheeks, as Donovan read the young man his rights.

As soon as he finished, Donovan slid a pad of paper and a pen across to Mark. "I'll need you to write down what happened, Mark. In the meantime, let me go talk to someone in the District Attorney's office and see what I can work out."

"Thank you," Suzie said.

Donovan walked over to the door and motioned to a uniformed cop to come over. "I want you in that room. That boy is writing a confession and no one – understand this, officer – no one is to enter that room until he is finished. Do you understand me?"

18

Donovan looked at his phone and swore. M. J. was calling again. He figured he better answer the call this time or hear about it later. "Marlie, I'm so sorry. I'm tied up right now. Can I call you back in a little while?" he blurted out, hoping to be able to put her off a little longer.

"What the hell is going on, Donovan?" Marla Jo yelled. "Do you know how many times I've tried to call you this afternoon?"

Donovan sighed. "Again, I'm sorry. But, I'm busy and I need to go. I'll call you later."

"Are Mark and Casey there?"

"Why?"

"My mother is going nuts worrying about them. She called me and said that you have them down there."

"I told you I was going to talk to them," Donovan reminded her.

"Couldn't you have just talked to them at their house? I don't understand why you had to haul them down there like they are criminals or something."

Donovan didn't respond, trying to figure out what to tell her. Now that Mark, Jr. had confessed, Donovan knew that Marla Jo would find out any minute now from her sister that he was being held. "Hold on a minute," he said, putting her on hold. He picked up his water bottle, took a huge swallow, set it down, and took Marla Jo off hold. "Are you still there?" he asked.

"I'm here," he said.

"Marlie, Mark, Jr. has been arrested. It seems that he decided. . ."

"What the hell do you mean, Mark's been arrested?

How could you do that? What the fuck is wrong with you?" Marla Jo screamed.

"Marlie, hold on," Donovan said, pulling the phone away from his ear. "Marlie! Stop shouting!" Donovan yelled. He waited a few seconds, hoping she would settle down. "Will you let me talk now?" he asked her when she didn't say anything.

"I don't know if I like it when you call me Marlie," she said softly. "It sounds weird coming from you."

"It feels weird saying it," Donovan replied. "Listen, I know how upsetting this is to you, but let me explain what happened here. Casey told the detective that was interviewing him that Mark, Jr. made a mixture from some berries he found."

"Found? I don't understand."

"His biology teacher taught the class all about different types of poisonous plants. Seeing as how so many kids spend time in the woods, they teach the kids what to look out for."

"Why do kids spend time in the woods? You're confusing me, Bobby."

"Hunting, fishing, camping, the boy scouts, the girl scouts, summer camps, and – I don't know – maybe bird watching. I guess these are all things that kids do around here."

"Really. Well, I never heard of my nephews doing any of that stuff. They are more into sports."

"Uh-huh. Anyway, Casey told the detective that his brother put some of the mixture into the wine that your dad drank. Mark wasn't trying to kill him. He didn't think it would do anything but get Frank sick. Mark thought it would be funny if his grandfather threw up on his birthday."

"Well, that's downright stupid."

"You're right. He's a stupid kid for doing it. However, I believe we have extenuating circumstances here, Marlie – um, M. J." He hesitated a moment. "Shit, now I don't know what to call you."

"So, what happens now?" She asked, ignoring his comment.

"He'll be held in juvy until he sees the judge tomorrow. Your sister is getting an attorney for him. Most likely he'll be released on his own recognizance. I've talked to the D.A. and I'm pretty sure a deal can be reached. I figure he'll get probation."

"You don't think he'll go to jail?"

"He probably won't have to do any jail time. His lawyer will probably plead accidental death. He's a minor and even if he has to serve time it would be done in a youth detention center."

"I'm sorry I yelled at you," Marla Jo told him.

"Forget it. I probably would have done the same thing if it was my nephew."

"Seriously, Bobby, how bad is it?"

"As I said, I think a deal will be made. I wouldn't worry too much about it."

"But, he'll have a record that will follow him forever," Marla Jo declared.

"Not necessarily so. He can always petition the court to have his records expunged or sealed. Don't worry. He'll be fine."

"I guess," she said.

Donovan heard her sigh. "How about dinner tonight?" he asked.

Marla Jo hesitated. "I think I'll spend some time with family tonight, Bobby. Maybe, I can put their minds at ease a little before tomorrow's hearing. After all, Mark will be spending the night behind bars. I'm sure they could use some moral support."

"You're right. I'll call you tomorrow."

"Night, Bobby," Marla Jo answered.

"Wait!" Donovan yelled, hoping to catch her before she ended the call.

"What?"

"Just to let you know, Mark isn't behind bars or being fed bread and water. He's spending the night in a pretty nice facility. I know he'll be scared, but you might want to let your sister know that he'll be well taken care of."

"Thanks, Bobby. I will," Marla Jo said. "Night."

Donovan threw his phone down on his desk. "Damn!" he uttered.

"Are you talking to yourself again, Donovan?" Detective Fritz asked, grinning.

"There are days that I hate this job," Donovan told him.

"Whatcha do now?"

"I just lied to a friend."

"Did you have a good reason?"

"What difference does that make? A lie is still a lie, good reason or not," Donovan said.

"Maybe. Maybe not. I figure it's okay to lie to keep from hurting someone's feelings. You know, like telling them their hair looks nice when it doesn't or things like that."

"Yeah? Well, how about when you tell someone that their nephew is probably going home and not to jail when you know it's a lie?" Donovan asked.

"That could come back to bite you in the ass. What's

the deal?"

"It's the McKnight case. It looks like his sixteen-year-old grandson poisoned him knowing very well that it could kill him. He said it was an accident, but there definitely was intent to at least make him ill."

"Maybe, he did think that whatever it was would only make him sick. That's just a boyish prank, isn't it?"

"Not when you know the poison is lethal," Donovan replied.

The detective stared at him. "He knew? Are you saying he killed the old man on purpose?"

"That's sure what it looks like to me," Donovan replied. "Even if they settle for involuntary manslaughter, that kid is looking at one to eight years behind bars."

"You know the D.A. isn't gonna do involuntary manslaughter if they can prove intent," the detective stated.

Donovan took a deep breath and let it out. "I'm screwed no matter what happens."

"Why is that? Because you lied to the kid's aunt? So what? We lie to people all the time."

"I know. But I like this woman. A lot," Donovan told him.

"Well, I'll be damned," Fritz said grinning. "You're in love."

"Knock it off, will you? I didn't say that," Donovan protested.

Fritz got up from his desk and looked around the squad room. "Hey, everyone!" he yelled, getting the attention of the rest of the cops in the room. "Guess what? A miracle happened. Donovan's in love!"

"Damn you, Fritz," Donovan yelled. "That's not funny."

"Wait! Wait!" Fritz called out, as the men in the room started jeering and making kissy sounds. "Who has 2019 in the pool?"

19

Detective Donovan looked up from the report he was reading and glanced over at the Stiverson murder board. Richard Stiverson was still first on his list of suspects with Roger Harper and Alex Morris coming in a close second and third.

David Freemont had been moved down a line to the middle of the board. Bella Francis, Mary Johanson, Janet Harper, and Alfred Freemont were now on the bottom of the board.

He was almost positive that the women could not be capable of murdering Barbara. Well, they might be capable of poisoning her, but he doubted they would have had the strength to cut her up.

David was a likely suspect but matricide was rare and, besides, Barbara wasn't expected to live much longer. All he had to do was wait a few more months for his mother to die and he would be a rich man. No logical reason to kill her, as far as Donovan could determine.

Alfred Freemont didn't need the money, so Donovan still wasn't sure why he convinced Barbara to take out a policy for a million dollars. The premiums had to have cost him a fortune over the past six years. Maybe, he decided to collect a little early? Still, he was pushing seventy and wasn't in good health. He would have needed some help chopping her up.

He stared at the picture of Roger Harper and frowned. Donovan had checked out his financials and it was clear that he was having money trouble. His business was about to go under and he certainly needed the $500,000.00 that he thought he was going to receive. I don't care for the man, Donovan thought. There's something off about him.

Alex Morris was also under the impression he was going to benefit from Barbara's death. After all, $250,000.00 isn't something to sneeze at. But, he has an alibi that seems legit.

Donovan removed Richard Stiverson's picture from the board. "I believe you belong up on the top," he mumbled, as he pinned it above Morris and Harper. He is about to inherit over one and a half million dollars, Donovan thought. Except for Barbara's kids, he definitely had the most to gain from Barbara's death. I think it's time we have another talk.

Two hours later, Richard Stiverson was sitting in an interview room, drumming his fingers on an old beat-up table. He checked his watch, stood up, and walked to the door. Suddenly, the door swung open, almost hitting him. "Watch it!" he yelled.

"Sorry," Donovan said, as he walked into the room.

"What the hell am I doing here, Detective? I've already told you everything I know about Barbara's death."

"Would you mind sitting down, Mr. Stiverson? I have a couple more questions I'd like to ask you."

Stiverson glared at him. "This is now reaching the point of harassment. Unless you have a good reason for hauling me down here once again, I'm leaving right now."

"I just told you, I have a few more questions. Now, would you please sit down?"

"No."

Donovan stared at him. "This will only take a few minutes, Mr. Stiverson."

"Am I under arrest, Detective?"

"Why? Should you be?" Donovan asked him.

"Funny man. So, am I?"

"No, you're not under arrest. At least, not at this time."

"Good. Then, I'm leaving. If you have any questions for me, call my attorney and set up an appointment." Stiverson opened the door and walked out.

Donovan watched him walk out of the room and smiled. "You prick," he muttered. "You so belong on the top of my list," he said.

Marla Jo glanced around the huge conference room and nodded her head. Everything looked okay. She anticipated that approximately twenty people would be attending this meeting, not including her and her boss, Maxwell Taylor.

After receiving numerous calls from various attorneys regarding the payouts of the insurance policies, it had been decided to have a joint meeting of all parties concerned. By doing this, all questions regarding the payouts could be addressed to the beneficiaries at the same time.

Ida opened the door to the conference and coughed.

"Yes?" Marla Jo asked, holding back a smile.

"There's a call for you," Ida told her.

"I asked you to hold my calls," Marla Jo reminded her.

"Yes, I remember, but I thought you might want to take this one. It's your man friend, Detective Donovan."

"Please tell him that I'll call him back," Marla Jo said.

"I did that already. He says it's important."

Marla Jo glanced at the clock on the wall. "All right. I'll be right back. Can you hold down the fort until I get back?"

"I'm sorry. Did you say something about holding some forks?" Ida asked her.

"No, I asked you to. . . Never mind. Just stay here and wait. Okay?"

"What am I waiting for?"

"Mr. Taylor, Ida. He will be here in a minute. Stay here and tell him that I'll be back in a minute. Can you do that?"

Ida smiled. "Well, of course, I can do that." She looked around the room. "Where do you keep them?"

Marla Jo looked confused. "Keep what?"

"The forks."

"Forget about the forks, Ida. I decided we won't need them after all," Marla Jo told her, rolling her eyes as she walked out of the room.

"This better be important, Bobby. I'm due in a meeting in a few minutes," Marla Jo told him as she picked up the phone.

"Hello to you, too," Donovan replied.

"Sorry. It's just that this isn't a good time."

"I won't keep you. I just wanted to give you a heads-up. I'm leaning towards Richard Stiverson as my main suspect."

"All right." She waited for Donovan to explain. "I think I knew that already. Is there anything else?" she finally asked when Donovan did not respond.

"I just wanted to remind you, in case. . ."

"What?" Marla Jo prompted when he didn't continue talking.

"Never mind. I'll let you go."

"Okay. Thanks for calling."

"One more thing," Donovan said.

"Yes?"

"What the hell do you want me to call you?"

Marla Jo laughed. "Is that the real reason you called me, Bobby? That couldn't wait?"

"I guess it could have But, it's bothering me, Ms. McKnight. A lot."

"I'll talk to you later. I've got to go. Bye, Bobby," Marla Jo said as she ended the call.

20

Marla Jo hurried back to the conference room just in time to see Ida asking people to take a seat. She motioned for Ida to come over to the doorway.

"I'm trying to seat people," Ida informed Marla Jo, a little out of breath as she ran over to the door.

"I can see that," Marla Jo replied.

"They're not sitting down."

"I'll take it from here, Ida. Thank you."

"Mr. Taylor hasn't shown up yet. Do you want me to go get him?"

"That's him coming now," Marla Jo said, seeing Taylor walking down the hall toward her.

Ida looked at the tall, white-haired man and smiled. "That's Mr. Taylor? He certainly is a looker," she said.

"I guess," Marla Jo agreed. "You can go back to work now."

"In a minute. I want to get a better look at him," Ida said. She stood up a little straighter and smiled.

"Maxwell, you're looking smart today," Marla Jo told him."

Ida stepped in front of Marla Jo and put out her hand. "It's so nice to meet you, Mr. Taylor. I'm Ida Itzie."

Taylor shook her hand. "Are you here for the meeting, Ms. Itzie?"

"Oh, my, no. And, please call me Ida. Is it okay if I call you Max?"

Taylor looked at Marla Jo. "Should I know this woman?" he asked.

"Sorry, Maxwell." She gently took Ida's arm and moved her out of the way. "You need to get back to work,

Ida," she said.

Ida smiled at Taylor. "It was nice meeting you, Max. I'm sure I'll see you again," she told him as she walked away.

"What was that all about?" Taylor asked.

"I think she has the hots for you, Maxwell."

"Does she work here?" he asked.

"She's temping for me until I find a permanent assistant," Marla Jo told him.

"She's a temp?" He laughed. "My God, the woman has to be a hundred years old.

"Doesn't make her any less horny," Marla Jo replied, grinning.

Taylor grinned. "If I ever get that desperate, kill me. Let's get this meeting over with, shall we?"

Maxwell Taylor took his place at the head of the conference table. "Ladies and gentlemen, would you please be seated." He watched as only a few people walked away from the large serving table that held coffee, tea, cold drinks, and several types of cookies and rolls. He turned to Marla Jo, who was standing next to him and shrugged. "It looks like they would rather eat."

"I've got it," she told him. "Unless you are all seated within the next thirty seconds, this meeting will be canceled," she shouted.

Stiverson turned and looked at the man standing next to him. "I told you she was a bitch," he said loud enough for the entire room to hear him.

Taylor waited until everyone was seated and then sat down. "First of all, if I hear any more disparaging remarks," he said, looking at Stiverson, "this meeting will be dismissed. Understood?" He waited. No one spoke.

"Good. I'd like to thank the representatives from AA Insurance and Superior Insurance for joining us today. I understand that some of you have brought your attorneys with you. I will be glad to answer any of your questions. I'm Maxwell Taylor, the CEO of Second Century Insurance Company. I believe most of you know Ms. McKnight." He looked at Marla Jo. "She is one of our insurance investigators and she has been assigned to the Barbara Stiverson case."

"Mr. Maxwell?"

Taylor looked at a woman sitting at the end of the table.

"It's Taylor, ma'am. Maxwell Taylor."

"Sorry."

"No problem. Is there something you wish to say?"

"Yes, Sir. My name is Mary Johanson and I was Barbara Stiverson's housekeeper. I was wondering if I could say something before you continue?"

"Of course."

"Thank you. First off, the policy that lists me as the beneficiary wasn't written by your company. I'm here for a different reason."

"And, what would that be?" Taylor asked.

"You know, I told Barbara more than once that I didn't want her insurance money, but she insisted on taking out that policy. I knew it was wrong and so did she. It was just as wrong as every other policy that she took out after she found out she was sick. The poor woman thought she was doing everyone a favor. God knows, her kids didn't need the insurance money."

"That was her idea," Bella interrupted. "We didn't ask her to do that."

"Just let me finish, Bella, and I'll be out of your

hair," Mary told her. "It made me sick watching those people coaxing her to take out those huge policies. Mr. Freemont, you already have a bundle of money but once you heard she had cancer – well, you rushed right over and asked her to give you a million dollars.

"I didn't know she was sick and I didn't ask her to give it to me. I paid those premiums."

"Yes, you did know and you figured she'd be dead in a couple of months. Less than two months after she was diagnosed, you were on her doorstep begging her to get a policy and name you as beneficiary. We all know you don't need more money. It was pure greed, plain and simple."

"Hey, I didn't do anything wrong. Don't lump me in with the rest of these vultures," Stiverson yelled out. "I had those policies long before she was sick. It was part of our divorce agreement."

"I wasn't referring to you, Mr. Stiverson," Mary said.

"All right, Mr. Stiverson, that's enough," Taylor said. He looked at Mary and smiled. "Mrs. Johanson, I want to thank you for coming here today. You have only confirmed what we already know to be true. We have the doctor's records and we know that Barbara was well aware of her condition before all of the life insurance policies were issued. Except, of course, for Mr. Stiverson's. I must say that I find it interesting that some of you showed up with your attorneys, thinking that it would make a difference. It won't. There is nothing they will be able to do for you to collect on these worthless policies. However, you may want to have them advise you on insurance fraud. It seems we have more than a few situations here where that has taken place."

"So, are we at least getting our money back?"

Freemont asked.

Taylor looked confused for a moment and then smiled. "Are you talking about the premiums you paid?"

"Exactly."

Taylor grinned. "I'm sorry, but no. In fact, we will be deciding if we are going to press charges against some of you."

As the bad news sunk in, several people started yelling threats about suing the insurance companies.

Taylor sat back in his chair, listening to the ruckus. Finally, having heard enough, he stood up. "That's enough. I suggest you lawyers get your clients under control," Taylor yelled. "This meeting is over." As he started towards the door, he looked at Mary Johanson. "Would you like to join me?" he asked.

Mary, looking scared, shook her head yes and walked over to him.

Taylor looked across the room at Marla Jo. "Already on it," she yelled to him.

Taylor took Mary's arm and started to escort her out of the room.

"Hold on, damn you," Richard Stiverson yelled to Taylor. "I want my money." He turned to his attorney. "Do something. What the hell am I paying you for?" Stiverson started to step closer to Taylor just as the security guards, Donald and Joe, walked into the room.

"Mr. Stiverson, are we going to have to escort you out of the building again?" Donald asked him, grinning.

"Get him out of here," Taylor shouted over his shoulder, as he walked out of the room.

"Hold on a minute, Donald," Marla Jo said, as she walked up to the security guard.

Stiverson gave her a dirty look. "What now?"

Ignoring him, Marla Jo looked at Stiverson's attorney. "Mr. - I'm sorry, we weren't introduced."

"Pollack. Anthony Pollack."

"Mr. Pollack, I've tried to explain this to Mr. Stiverson but he doesn't seem to understand. Could you please explain to him why we cannot release any funds until the police investigation is over?"

"Well, I don't get it either, Ms. McKnight. Barbara Stiverson took those policies out in 1997 and 1998. She wasn't ill at the time and I also think that my client should be paid."

"We know when the policies were taken out and Mr. Stiverson will be paid in due time, as long as he is cleared of Barbara's death."

Pollack stared at her. "You mean he's still a suspect in her murder?"

"He's one of many. Did he neglect to tell you that part of the story, Mr. Pollack?"

Pollack stared at Stiverson. "Richard, didn't you think that was pertinent? I was under the impression you weren't a suspect any longer."

"I didn't have nothing to do with her murder," Stiverson yelled.

"Ms. McKnight, exactly why was this meeting held today? As far as I'm concerned, it was a waste of time."

"Are you kidding, Mr. Pollack? This meeting was held as a courtesy to you and your client and everyone else that was here today. We hoped that it would put a stop to the endless phone calls we have been receiving demanding money. To tell you the truth, I was against this meeting. However, Mr. Taylor thought it would help if we could explain to everyone what was going on."

"Of course, she was against it," Stiverson

interrupted. "I told you she's a. . ."

Donald stepped next to Stiverson. "I wouldn't finish that sentence if I was you."

"You're right, Mr. Pollack," Marla Jo continued, still ignoring Stiverson. "It was a waste of time. So, please take your rude-ass client and get out. I'll let you know what we decide when the time comes and not one minute before."

Stiverson glared at her. "You better watch your back, McKnight or you just might end up like your father."

Marla Jo took a step back and looked at Donald. "I do believe that was a threat, Donald. Perhaps we should detain Mr. Stiverson until the police get here."

Pollack grabbed Stiverson's arm and started walking rapidly towards the door. "No need for the police. He was just letting off a little steam," he told Marla Jo.

"Let go of me," Stiverson yelled at Pollack as he pulled his arm loose. "You're fired, you good-for-nothing piece of shit."

Within the blink of an eye, Donald had Stiverson by the back of the neck and was pushing him toward the door.

"I'm sorry," Pollack told Marla Jo. "I really am sorry."

"So am I." Marla Jo replied. "Next time you have a meeting, you should be sure you have all the facts before you start mouthing off."

21

"You said. . . You told me. . ." Marla Jo was sobbing so hard she couldn't finish her sentence.

Donovan pulled her close and held her while she cried on his shoulder. "I'm so sorry. I had no idea that the D.A. would go for first-degree murder," he told her.

Marla Jo pushed away from him and wiped her eyes. "You said maybe probation, Bobby. How could you have been so far off?"

"I didn't know the D.A. would go that far. Seriously, I didn't," Donovan protested. "I figured accidental death is what they would charge him with. However, the fact that he knew the berries were poisonous and would most likely kill your dad. . . Well, it does look like he killed him on purpose."

Marla Jo stared at him. "How can you say that? Mark doesn't have a mean bone in his body."

Donovan frowned. "I'm sorry, but he kinda does or he wouldn't have done this."

Marla Jo sighed. "Can I sit down?"

"Of course," Donovan replied, as he pulled a chair away from the table.

"This is killing my sister, you know. My whole family is devastated. He's going to spend years behind bars, isn't he, Bobby?"

"We'll see. I'm going to ask the D.A. to try him as a juvenile."

"What do you mean?" Marla Jo asked, looking shocked. "Are they planning to try him as an adult?"

"I'm afraid so," Donovan told her, grimacing as she lost all control and started sobbing again. "Would you like some water?" he asked after a few moments.

Marla Jo shook her head yes. "And. . . and, a tissue," she mumbled through her sobs. "I need a tissue."

"I'll be right back," Donovan said.

Marla Jo looked up as Donovan walked back into the room. "I'm sorry I lost it. I'm such a baby," she told him.

"You have nothing to apologize for, M. J. I'm the one who should be apologizing to you. I gave you false hope, but I truly didn't think it would go this far. There is good news, though."

Marla Jo wiped her red swollen eyes and tried to smile. "I could use some of that. What is it?"

"The D.A. isn't pressing charges against Casey."

"What do you mean?" she asked looking confused. "Why would. . . I don't get it."

"There was some talk about Casey being an accessory to the murder. He knew what his brother was doing but he didn't say anything or try to stop him. In all actuality, he was a party to his grandfather's death, but the D.A.'s office is going to overlook the part he played. He won't even get probation as long as he cooperates with the D.A.'s office."

Marla Jo looked shocked, her mouth hanging open as she listened to what Donovan was telling her. "Are you saying he has to testify against Mark?"

"I'm afraid so."

"I can't listen to any more of this, Bobby. It's too much. I'm leaving," as she stood up.

"I'm sorry I upset you. Let me give you a ride. I don't think you should drive right now."

"I'm fine." She looked around the room, looking

confused.

"Is something wrong?"

"I'm looking for my purse. I'm sure I had it with me."

"It's on your arm." He took her hand and held on to it. "Come with me. I'm taking you home."

"I'm fine."

"No, you're not."

Two hours later, Detective Donovan slid into a booth at Mabel's Diner.

"Whataya having, Sweetie?" the waitress asked, as she strolled up to him, holding a pot of coffee.

He looked at the coffee. "Some of that," he told her. "And, keep it coming."

"Long day, Sugar?" she asked as she poured his coffee.

"You have no idea and it's gonna get a lot longer," Donovan replied, smiling. "How's the Reuben?"

"Best in town," she told him.

"I have that with fries and make those fries extra crispy."

"Coming right up," she said, as she walked away.

Donovan looked across the booth and frowned. "You said you have something to tell me."

"I do."

Donovan took a sip of his coffee. "I'm waiting."

"I lied to you about where I was when Barbara was murdered."

"I see," Donovan replied.

"You don't seem surprised."

"Not much surprises me. People lie. That's what they do."

"I was with Bella."

"I know. She told me."

"What the fuck, man? She told you? You knew?"

"I knew from the minute you told me where you were when Barbara Stiverson was killed that you were lying. You're a terrible liar, by the way. Plus, it was obvious that your so-called friends were covering for you."

"Then why didn't you say something?"

"What for? Bella provided you with an alibi. I could give a rat's ass where you were as long as you weren't in that house slicing up that poor woman. Her husband doesn't know about you two, so why start trouble with the two of them if I don't have to."

Alex Morris sat back in the booth and stared at Donovan. "There's more."

"Thank you," Donovan said, as the waitress put his food down on the table in front of him. "Looks great."

"Tastes even better, Sugar. "Anything else you need right now?"

"Don't think so," Donovan said, as he reached for the ketchup bottle. "Fries look great."

Morris watched as Donovan piled the ketchup on top of his fries and started eating. "You want one?" he asked Morris, as he shoved a couple of fries into his mouth.

"I don't eat greasy foods, but thanks."

"So, what's the more?" Donovan asked.

"I think her brother killed her."

"Really? Why do you think that?"

"He's broke. He needs money. I think he killed her for the insurance money."

"Well, he's shit out of luck there, isn't he?" Donovan said as he chewed his food. "Do you have any proof?"

"No, but I think it must be him."

"I don't think he's physically capable of it," Donovan said.

"Maybe. But, what if he had help?"

Donovan took a huge bite of his sandwich, chewed a couple of times, and washed it down with a gulp of coffee. "Look, Morris, if you know something, spit it out. You're wasting my time with this cat-and-mouse game you're playing."

Alex Morris smiled. "I spent a lot of time in that house, Detective. I was there when he convinced Barbara to take out those insurance policies. They fought about money all the time. There was this one time when they got into a huge fight and he threatened her and, sick as she was, she slapped him. Hard. I mean really hard, man. And, you know what he did?" Morris asked Donovan, waiting for a reply.

Donovan sighed. "What?"

"He slapped her back. She had bruises on her face for weeks. That was when she told him to stay away from her. He stormed out of that house, yelling threats all the way down the driveway. He did it all right," Morris said, looking pleased with himself. "You can bet your bottom dollar on it."

Donovan didn't say anything, thinking about what Morris had told him. "Is there anyone who can back this up? You know, what you've just told me. Was anyone else aware of this?" he asked after a few moments.

"Barbara must have told someone - her kids or her sister. Mary Johanson was there every day so she must have seen the bruises."

"Anything else?" the waitress interrupted. "More coffee or how about some dessert?"

"I'm good," Donovan told her. "Just the check,

please."

She laid the check on the table in front of Donovan. "You can pay up front."

"Thanks," Donovan said, as he pushed the check over to Morris. "You got this, right?" he asked, as he got out of the booth. "I'll be in touch."

Morris watched him as he walked out of the diner. "Son of a bitch," he muttered as he picked up the check and looked at it.

22

"I told you not to call me."

"Like I give a shit what you say. I need money," Sam yelled. "We're starving here."

"I told you, I don't have it."

"Don't give me that crap. I know you have money."

"Not that much."

"You promised me $10,000.00 if I helped you out. I want it or else," Sam shouted.

"Or else what? From where I'm standing, I don't see that there is a whole lot you can do about it."

"A thousand dollars. I'll take a thousand right now. You can pay me the rest later."

"I don't have it."

"Listen, you either give me some money or I'm going to the cops. Charlie and me are hungry. We need food. I'm broke. I can't pay my electric bill. I know you've got money."

"You're not going to the cops, Sam. They'll throw your ass in jail and then who is going to take care of your precious Charlie?"

Sam was quiet. "I might," he muttered after a few moments.

"No, you won't. Now stop bothering me. You'll get your money when I get mine."

"Not good enough." He hesitated a moment. "You do realize I know where you live, don't you?"

"Is that a threat?"

"You damn right it is," Sam replied. "And, right now I'm thinking you might not taste too bad."

"Okay. Okay. You don't have to get all nasty on me.

I can buy you some groceries, but that's about it."

"Really? That's what you can do? Forget it. I want five hundred dollars today or else. Put it in an envelope and drop it in my mailbox. Understand?"

"Two-fifty."

"Five hundred. I'm done negotiating, you idiot," Sam yelled. "In one hour or else. If that money ain't in my mailbox in one hour, one of two things is gonna happen. Either I go to the cops and tell them what you did or – depending on how hungry I am – I'm gonna slice you open and eat your fucking liver. Got it?"

23

"Hey, Donovan, are you still working on that Stiverson case?"

Donovan glanced over at a fellow detective sitting at a desk across the room from him. "Yeah. Why?"

"There some cop from the 8th precinct that wants to talk to the guy in charge. Line four."

"Thanks," Donovan said, as he picked up the phone. "Detective Donovan here," he said.

"Hey, man. It's Willy, Donovan. How the hell you doing?"

"Willy Richards? My God, it's been ages since I talked to you?"

"Time flies when you're having fun."

"So, how are things over at the 8th?"

"I've been busier than a mosquito at a nudist colony. I swear this crap never slows down."

"Are you calling to say hi or is it business?" Donovan asked.

"It's both, but mostly business. Hence, the reason for the call."

"Hence?" Donovan repeated, laughing.

"You heard me. Hence. It fits. Look it up."

"I might just do that. So, why are you calling?"

"We've had a sizable increase of break-ins in the area in the past few weeks. That wouldn't be so unusual except the only stuff being taken is food."

"Are just houses being robbed?"

"Yeah," Willy replied. "Well, no. Actually, a few restaurants have reported some losses, too. They're probably connected."

"What kind of food? Meat and canned goods?"

"You hit the nail on the head, Bobby. So, I guess it's true then?"

"What's true?"

"About the Stiverson woman who was murdered and cut to pieces. I heard that there was food missing from her freezer," Richards told him.

"Weirdest damn thing ever. Just some canned goods and a few frozen packages of meat were taken. There was jewelry and some really expensive items in that house that could have been pawned, but none of that was missing."

"Anywho, Donovan, we ran some of the prints we gathered from these places that had food missing and we found a match. Don't have a frickin' name but we found a match in the database and guess what?"

Donovan rolled his eyes. "Tell me," he said, wishing Willy would get to the point.

"It seems you might be looking for the same guy that we are. Our prints match some of the prints you took from that Stiverson house. How do you like those cookies?"

"I think I like them just fine," Donovan told him, interested now as he sat up a little straighter in his chair. "If it is the same guy, it seems he's pretty damn hungry."

"I'd say so," Willy agreed. "Probably homeless."

"Homeless? You think so?" Donovan asked.

"I'd say so. Or, close to it."

"Yeah, maybe, Willy. But if he was homeless he wouldn't be stealing frozen meat, would he? He'd have to have a place to cook it, too. Nope, I don't think he's' homeless. Down on his luck? Definitely. But, he's not homeless."

"You could be right Anyway, we're still checking the shelters to see if anyone has shown up with any kind of food."

"Good luck with that," Donovan said.

"Thanks. I'll let you know if we get a hit with the prints or whatever else."

"Thanks, Willy, I appreciate it."

"One more thing, Donovan."

"What's that?"

"I heard that you're missing some of Stiverson's body parts. Do you figure our guy took those, too?"

"It looks that way," Donovan replied.

"Didn't have to wait for those to thaw out, did he? They were nice and fresh."

"Are you suggesting he ate them? That's kinda gross, don't you think?"

"What do you think he did with them?" Willy asked.

"How the hell should I know? And, Willy?"

"Yeah?"

"Next time you want to talk about eating people parts, don't call me at lunchtime. Okay?"

Willy laughed. "Got it. You'll let me know if you find out anything. Right?"

"Absolutely. You'll be the first person I call," Donovan replied.

"Well, I won't keep you. I've got people to see, things to do, and places to go, you know," Richards said laughing. "Over and out."

Donovan chuckled as he hung up his phone. "The guy is nuttier than a fruitcake," he mumbled. But, he is one hell of a cop, he thought as he picked up the phone to make a call.

"Hi, Bobby."

"I'm sorry it took so long to get back to you. It's been a crazy morning."

"Here, too. Anyway, just so you know, Mark Jr. didn't poison my dad."

Donovan sighed. "I know you don't want to accept it, but he confessed, M. J."

"Well, he's wrong. He may think he did it, but I have proof he didn't do it."

"Really? And, what would that be?"

"The berries he picked aren't poisonous. I had them checked out and the biologist said there was no way they could have killed my dad. He didn't do it, Bobby," she exclaimed.

"Hold on. Let's back up a little. How do you know what berries he picked?"

"You hold on a minute. First of all, you don't have a sample of the wine that was supposedly poisoned. The glass he drank from was washed and the bottle somehow disappeared. So, as far as we know, the wine wasn't poisoned."

"It had to be," Donovan protested.

"There's more. Mrs. Billington - you remember her, don't you?"

"Mark's biology teacher."

"Right. Well, Mrs. Billington, Casey, Mark's lawyer, and I went for a walk in the woods. Perhaps that's something you should have done? Anyway, Casey took us right to the bushes with the berries that Mark picked. Mark thought he was picking pokeberries, which can make you sick, but they were elderberries, Bobby. They look pretty much the same, but elderberries are smaller and perfectly round. Mrs. Billington explained it all to us.

Mark said he didn't think the berries he picked would kill anybody, just make them sick. But, he picked elderberries, Donovan, and they don't make you sick."

Donovan took a deep breath and let it out. "You do realize that I can't just take your word for this. I'm going to have to have forensics check all this out, you know."

"Don't sound so happy," Marla Jo retorted. "This is good news, you know. And, I want you to check it out."

"Sorry. Of course, it's good news. However, if Mark didn't kill your father. . ."

"Yes?"

"Well, then, who the hell did?"

Marla Jo didn't say anything, thinking about Donovan's question.

"Are you still there?" Donovan finally asked.

"I'm thinking."

"And?"

"What if my father wasn't poisoned at all? We know what Mark did, but that didn't kill him. Neither did the poop. If there was poison in his system it had to come from something else. Do you agree?"

"I don't know. Donovan answered reluctantly. "I guess."

"And, what if the coroner did make a mistake? Anyway, the family has decided that we want another autopsy."

Donovan took a deep breath and let it out. "You're kidding."

"We have the right, don't we?"

"Yes, M. J., but it's a waste of time," he said, getting irritated. "And money," he added.

"It's our money," Marla Jo snapped. "I want a copy of the autopsy report. Did your guy even check out anything besides his blood?"

"Of course, he did. He did a complete examination of the body and organs. And, he's the county coroner, not my guy."

"How complete a job did he do, Donovan?"

"I've seen the report. There was poison in his system!" he yelled.

"You know what?" Marla Jo said softly. "I think he had a heart attack and that's what killed him. We're doing another autopsy."

"Good God, M. J. He's been buried. You'll have to dig him up."

"Which is why we have to do it now, while he's still fresh," she declared.

"What if you do this and find out it was all for nothing? Then what?"

"Then we'll put his sorry ass back in his coffin and bury him again. But, one way or the other, Bobby, we need to know that nothing was overlooked."

Donovan sighed. "Is everyone in your family on board with this?" He waited. "M. J.?"

"Mostly. Pete and Mom weren't too crazy about the idea so we voted. Digging him up won out. It's gonna happen, Donovan."

24

"Freemont's in trouble," Detective Fritz told Donovan as he sat down at his desk.

Donovan looked over at him and frowned. "What do you mean he's in trouble?"

"He's practically broke. I ran a check on his financials like you asked and it isn't looking good."

"Explain, please," Donovan said.

Fritz looked down at the paper he was holding and said, "It started a couple of years ago when he started gambling. Well, maybe it was more than a couple."

Donovan held up a hand. "Wait. When did it start exactly?"

"Around 2010 or 2011. I'd say more like 2010. He started going to Vegas a few times a year. It escalated to a couple of times a month. He bet big and he lost a lot of money. Also, around that same time, he bought a couple of racehorses. They cost him a fortune and within six months both were put down due to injuries."

"How much money are you talking about?" Donovan asked.

Fritz turned the paper over and shook his head. "Who knew that horses were so expensive? He spent almost half a mil on the two."

"Didn't he have insurance on them?"

"I couldn't find that he did and I didn't find any big deposit from any insurance company after the horses died."

"And, Vegas?" Donovan inquired. 'How much?"

"Almost all his liquid assets. He still has his house and some of his cars, but most of the cash is gone."

"How much, Fritz?"

"It looks like he blew at least three point five."

Donovan sat back in his chair, a shocked look on his face. "Million?"

"That's right," Fritz declared. "It looks like he has about two or three hundred thousand left. Cash that is. I'm still looking into his stocks and stuff, but I think he's already cashed most of that in."

"Well, I'll be damned," Donovan declared, grinning. "We have a motive. He needed the money. Plus, his alibi for where he was the day Barbara Stiverson was murdered didn't check out. We might just have our man, Fritz."

"You think? Here's the part that doesn't make sense to me, Donovan."

"What?"

"He had Barbara Stiverson take that policy out in 2013. Right?"

"Right. So?" Donovan asked.

"He still had a lot of money then. He didn't need the million dollars."

"Maybe he was trying to make up for the losses he suffered from those horses. He probably figured Barbara wouldn't be around much longer and he would recoup his losses. You know, even out."

Fritz scratched the top of his head. "I guess that could be it." He shook his head, getting excited now. "Of course. That makes sense. He's been waiting for years for that money but now he really needs it. He's going broke. So he kills her for the money." He gave Donovan a questioning look. "Do you think he did it?"

"I think we should at least have another discussion with him and find out just where the hell he was that day."

"Didn't he ever tell you where he was? I mean, he had to have told you something?"

Donovan laughed. "Oh, he did, all right. He said he was visiting his mother."

Fritz stared at him. "His what?" he finally said.

"That's right," Donovan told him, grinning. "He said he was visiting his mother in her assisted living facility."

"How old is Freemont, anyway?" Fritz asked him.

"He's in his seventies. His mother is ninety-seven years old, practically blind, can't hear for shit, and uses one of those things with wheels to walk. When I went to see her to confirm Freemont's alibi, she wasn't sure if he had visited her or not. Plus – get this, Fritz – no one working there could verify his story either. It seems they don't keep track of visitors if they are family. So, who knows if he was there or not?"

"You know he's pretty old to be chopping someone up, don't you?"

"I do know that. I think he had help. I just don't know who yet."

"So, watcha gonna do now?"

"As I said, I think it's time to have another talk with Mr. Freemont. Do you want to go get him or should I send Officer Chesterton?"

"I'd like to keep working on this if you don't mind."

"All right. Chesterton it is."

Alfred Freemont looked exactly like Wilford Brimley, the actor. He even sounded like him, which tended to make Donovan forget who he was talking to. He looked across the table at the man and smiled. "Thanks for coming in to see me," Donovan said.

Freemont gave him a dirty look. "I didn't have much choice, did I?"

Donovan shrugged. "Guess not." He shuffled some papers around, found what he was looking for, and looked over at Freemont. "It seems you have a couple of problems, Mr. Freemont."

Freemont stared at him for a second. "Really?"

"Yes, really. It seems that no one remembers that you visited your mother the day that Barbara Stiverson was murdered."

Freemont continued to stare at Donovan, not responding to his statement.

"Well?" Donovan asked.

"Well, what?" Freemont replied.

"I'd like to know where you were that day. After one-thirty in the afternoon. You were not visiting your mother."

"Prove it," Freemont responded and reached into his shirt pocket and pulled out a pack of cigarettes. Staring at Donovan, he pulled one out of the pack and put it in his mouth.

"You can't smoke in here," Donovan said.

"I know that. I'm not lighting it."

"Mr. Freemont, exactly where were you the afternoon that your ex-wife was murdered?"

Freemont sat back in his chair and frowned. "Exactly why am I here, Detective? I've already had this discussion with you and you know where I was."

"No one can back up your story. Plus, you are practically broke. Bad investments and gambling can do that, as you well enough know. You need money and you were tired of waiting for Barbara to die, so you decided to help her along. Isn't that right?"

Freemont looked him in the eye. "As I said, prove it, Detective. This is bullshit. You're fishing here and I'm not biting. Now, if you'll excuse me, I've got better things to do with my time than sit here with you and listen to nonsense."

"We're not done, Mr. Freemont."

"Maybe you're not, but I am. If you have anything else to say about this business, call my attorney."

Donovan watched as the old man pushed his chair away from the table and stood up. "Who helped you, Freemont?"

Freemont glanced over at him. "What are you talking about?"

"An old man like you. . . Well, I figured you had to have help. After all, cutting up a body is hard work. So, who helped you? Was it Roger? Or, maybe it was David?" Donovan smirked. "It was Roger, wasn't it? You and Roger killed that poor woman thinking you'd get all that money and it was all for nothing."

Freemont walked to the door, opened it, turned, and looked back at Donovan. "God, you're stupid. How do you even keep a job?"

25

Marla Jo stood in the doorway that connected her room to her secretary's office, getting more upset by the minute. Where the hell is she, she wondered. She's been gone for over thirty minutes. She was about to walk back to her desk when the door opened and Ida walked into the room.

"Where have you been? The phone has been ringing off the hook," Marla Jo asked.

Ida jumped and put her hand over her heart. "You almost gave me a heart attack," she told Marla Jo.

"I'm sorry, Ida, but I was beginning to think you had gone home or something. Where were you?"

"Bathroom break. You know it takes a little longer when you're my age. Plus, I wanted to say hi to Maxwell."

"No, Ida. You must not bother Mr. Taylor. He's a very busy man. I've told you this a million times."

Ida straightened up and stared at Marla Jo. "Well, I don't think I'm doing anything wrong if I just go say hi now and then. He's very nice to me. I think he likes me."

"He likes everyone and he's nice to everyone. Please, Ida, just quit bothering him." Marla Jo glanced at the phone on Ida's desk, which was begging to be answered. "Please get that, will you?"

"Whatever you say, miss."

Marla Jo sighed and went back into her office.

"It's your detective friend," Ida yelled as Marla Jo started to close the door. "Do you want to talk to him?"

"I'll take it," Marla Jo told her as she shut the door and walked over to her desk. "Donovan?" she snapped as she picked up her phone.

"Whoa! You don't have to yell. Did I call at a bad time?"

"I'm sorry. It's Ida. And, before you say anything, I know I need to get a new secretary. But, that woman is driving me nuts."

"What did she do now?"

"Forget it. It's not important." Marla Jo took a deep breath and let it out. "Sorry. Now, what can I do for you?"

"Freemont just moved up to the top of the suspect list. I thought you might like to know."

Marla Jo sat back in her chair and frowned. "Are you serious?"

"Sure am. He had the motive and he doesn't have an airtight alibi for the time that Barbara Stiverson was murdered."

"Come on, Donovan. There's no way that old man could have chopped her up."

"We figure he had help. Perhaps, Roger Harper."

"Her brother?" Marla Jo exclaimed. "No way."

"They are both broke and neither one can account for his time when. . ."

"Harper was working. You know that. His customers verified that he was in his shop during the time of the murder. And, if you recall, his girlfriend also said he was there. Ugh!"

"What, ugh?"

"I still can't imagine him having a girlfriend. Just the sight of him gives me the creeps."

"Well, truthfully, I am kinda iffy about Harper. David might have helped Freemont though."

"You're reaching, Donovan, and you know it. The doctor confirmed that David had been ill for days before his mother was murdered. He had the mumps, for crying out loud.

"I know that's what the doctor said. You don't think he was covering for him, do you?" Donovan replied.

Marla Jo rolled her eyes and sighed.

"I heard that," Donovan said.

"Good. Anything else you're imagining that you want to share?"

"Funny girl," Donovan muttered.

"Hey? What about Janet?" Marla Jo asked. "Did you ever check her story out?"

"Of course. She was in St. Thomas on vacation."

"For sure?"

"For sure."

"It looks like your suspect list has been narrowed down to two," Marla Jo told him. "Let's hope it turns out to be Stiverson. That would sure save our company a whole bunch of money."

"I don't think he was the one, M. J." He was quiet for a moment. "Unless he got someone to drive his car to the lake, he was probably fishing just like he said. We checked his fishing gear and the line on the reel was still wet."

"What are you talking about?" Marla Jo asked. "Wet. What does that mean?"

"I used to go fishing with my dad. When we'd come home he would string out the fishing line and make sure it was clean and dry before he reeled it back onto the spool. It helps to make the line last longer. Anyway, Stiverson's line was still pretty damp when we checked it. I think he was fishing just like he said"

"Shit!" Marla Jo exclaimed. "Well, that leaves one."

"It does. Freemont is looking better all the time. Now I've just got to figure out who helped him."

"You know, Donovan, if he did have help it doesn't necessarily have to be anyone on your list. You could be dealing with an unknown."

"You could be right. I don't think Freemont worked alone and I don't think we have any idea who helped him. He's not going to crack no matter how many times I interview him."

"Listen, Donovan, I've got to go. The phone calls are backing up here. Can I call you later?"

"How about dinner?"

"I'll call you later."

Donovan pulled the phone away from his ear and looked at it. "Damn, she's a rude woman," he uttered. He hung up his phone and turned his chair towards the murder board behind his desk. He stood up, walked over to it, and started moving all the pictures except Freemont's to the bottom of the board. He hesitated when he started to remove Stiverson's picture. "Do I leave you on top or not?" he asked quietly.

He removed the picture from the board and stared at it.

"Wishing isn't going to make it so."

Donovan jumped and turned to see who was behind him. "Damn you, Fritz. Stop sneaking up on people."

"He goes on the bottom with the rest of them," Fritz told him.

"I know."

"So, Freemont is your man?"

"I'm pretty sure. Now, I just have to prove it."

26

"My sister doesn't like you, you know."

Donovan looked over at her, shrugged, and took a bite of pizza. "That's her problem."

"You lied to her. She doesn't like liars."

"I didn't know it would turn out to be a lie."

"Yes, you did. You're lying to me right now. You are a liar, aren't you, Donovan?" Marla Jo asked.

"Maybe, when I have to be. I guess I do lie when I'm working. You know, when I'm interrogating a suspect. It's part of the job."

"Are you working right now?"

Donovan grinned. "Yes."

Marla Jo stared at him. "I thought this was a date, numbnuts."

"It is. And, you are a lot of work."

"Funny."

"I'll try to make it up to your sister somehow. Do you think I should send her a box of candy?"

Marla Jo grinned. "You are really something, you know that? And, no. No candy. She's on a diet and that would upset her. Flowers would be better."

"Besides, it all turned out okay. Your nephews are off the hook."

"No thanks to you," Marla Jo said as she took a sip of beer and burped.

"Nice," Donovan commented.

"Sorry. Excuse me."

"You're excused."

"Have you figured out who killed my dad yet?"

"I think it was your mom."

Marla Jo threw her half-eaten slice of pizza down on her plate. "What the hell is wrong with you? You know it wasn't her."

Donovan smiled. "It might have been. And, no. I haven't figured it out yet."

"Well, maybe the autopsy will tell us something new."

Donovan frowned. "Are you going to go through with that? I thought it was just talk."

"Nope. We are exhuming the body, Donovan. It's scheduled for tomorrow."

"It seems like a lot of trouble and expense to go to for nothing."

"Your opinion," Marla Jo mumbled as she took another bite of pizza.

"Do you like this pizza?"

"I think it's about the best in town. Don't you think so?"

"I do, although Mama's Pizza may be better. By the way, you never mentioned what happened with that subpoena you got. Did it turn out to be anything important?"

Marla Jo glanced over at him and shook her head. "Not really. It's kinda a moot point anyway."

Donovan studied her face for a moment. "I didn't mean to upset you. What was it for?"

"I'm not upset. My father was being sued. It seems he got into a fight with a couple of guys and there was some property damage and the owner was suing him to get reimbursed."

"What did that have to do with you?"

"The attorney for the man who had the damage to his property wanted me to testify in court for his client.

He wanted me to testify that my dad had a really bad temper. I refused. I told him I wouldn't say anything bad about my father and, therefore, I was served that subpoena. But, now that dad's gone, the whole thing has been dropped. I was concerned that they would try to get the money from dad's estate, but Mr. Knowles knows my mom and he said to forget about it."

"Well, that was nice of him. So, what was the fight about, anyway?"

"Same old crap. Men's egos, too much booze, too much testosterone and. . ."

"Wait a minute," Donovan interrupted. "Did that fight take place in a bar?"

"Yeah. Kelsey's."

"You told me that Stiverson said he knew your dad from drinking together at Kelsey's."

"You're right." She thought for a moment. "That's where the fight took place. Dad usually only went to one bar and it was Kelsey's."

"And, Stiverson and your dad were drinking buddies."

"At one time, perhaps. However, not anymore from what Stiverson said. But, it doesn't make sense, Donovan. If the fight was at Kelsey's, why would dad continue drinking there? Would Knowles even let him in the door if he was suing him?"

"Who knows, lassie? We Irish are a strange but lovable lot."

Marla Jo laughed. "Strange – yes. Lovable? Well, that is definitely debatable."

"I'd like to talk to your mom," Donovan said.

"Why? You gonna arrest her now?"

"Seriously, M. J., I'd like to talk to her."

"Now?"

"It's early. Is she still up?"

"Let me call her and see if she wants company."

Donovan stood up. "I'm gonna go see a man about a horse. I'll be right back."

"Are you sure it isn't too late? I could wait and talk to her tomorrow," Donovan asked Marla Jo as they got into his car.

"She said to come over. I still don't know what you think she's gonna be able to tell you."

"Maybe nothing. But, I've got this feeling that she may be able to help."

"Help what? You solve my dad's murder?"

"Exactly."

Marla Jo looked over at him wondering what was going through that mind of his. She let out a deep sigh, put her head back, and closed her eyes. "Wake me when we get there," she mumbled.

Donovan glanced over at her and smiled. "Will do," he told her.

"What can I get you to drink?" Betsy asked Donovan and her daughter as they settled into the comfortable living room couch. "Coffee? Wine? Beer?"

"Coffee would be great, Mom," Marla Jo said. "I need to wake up."

"You work too hard, Marlie. You need to get more rest."

"I get plenty of rest, Mom."

"I don't think so. If you did you wouldn't be so tired. Isn't that right, Detective Donovan?"

"Please, Mrs. McKnight, call me Robert."

"I think we've done this dance before, Robert. And, I'm Betsy."

"Right," Donovan replied smiling.

"How about we go to the kitchen?" Betsy said. "The coffee is fresh and it's so much homier in there."

Donovan stood and reached out for Marla Jo's hand. "Come on, Sleepy," he said, as he pulled her up off the couch.

"You don't have any cookies, do you?" Marla Jo asked as she walked into the kitchen and sat down at the table.

"Don't I always?" Betsy said. "So, Robert, what is so important that it couldn't wait until tomorrow?"

Donovan gave Marla Jo a questioning look. "Is that what you told your mom?"

She grinned and shrugged.

"I'm sorry, Betsy. It could have waited."

"No, no," Betsy said. "It's fine. In fact, I'm glad to have a little company."

"Are you doing okay? I know it must be difficult for you," Donovan said.

"I'm doing fine." She poured the coffee, sat down, and smiled at Donovan. "So, what can I do for you?"

"Wait," Marla Jo cried out. "Cookies."

"You know where they are," Betsy told her and looked back at Donovan.

"Are you familiar with Kelsey's Bar and Grill?"

Betsy smiled. "Of course. Frank and I have been going there for years. Well, more so Frank the past few years. I hardly went anymore. Frank wasn't real nice when he drank and sometimes he would get nasty to me in front of the other people and.... Well, I just figured it would be better to stay home."

"So, you know the owner of the bar, Knowles?"

"Of course. Jimmy and I go way back. We dated in high school. He was a few years older than me and after he graduated high school he went into the service. We lost touch for a while. Now, we're just old friends who see each other now and then."

"You never told me that," Marla Jo stated.

"There's a lot of things I never told you," her mother said.

"Is he married?" Donovan inquired.

"He was. He lost his wife a few years ago,"

"Do you think he still has feelings for you?" Donovan asked.

"What?" Betsy exclaimed, looking surprised. "Of course not. Why would you think that?" Betsy stared at Donovan. "What are you getting at, Robert?"

"Please, Betsy, bear with me. You'll see where this is heading."

Betsy sighed. "All right."

"Do you know a man named Richard Stiverson?"

Betsy looked surprised. "How do you know him?"

"So, you do know him?"

"I do. He's a rotten person. He has a foul mouth and a horrible temper. He got into a fight with Frank a while back. He and another man named Percy something. They did a lot of damage to Jimmy's bar."

"Jimmy was suing Frank for damages. Right?" Donovan continued.

"Yes. How do you know all this?"

"How long ago was the fight, Betsy," Donovan asked, ignoring her question.

Betsy thought for a moment. "Probably four or five months ago."

"However, Frank kept drinking at the bar. Right?"

"Right. Jimmy wasn't part of the fight, so he didn't care if Frank kept coming in as long as he didn't start any more fights. He figured he'd get his money eventually, so Frank being there wasn't a problem for him."

"And, Stiverson kept drinking there after the fight, also?"

"As far as I know," Betsy told him. "You'd need to ask Jimmy."

"How was Frank feeling the past few months before he died?" Donovan asked, changing the subject.

"How do you mean?" Betsy inquired, again looking confused.

"Did he complain about not feeling well, stomach pains, anything like that?"

Betsy thought for a moment. "Frank wasn't one to complain much," she said. "Isn't that right, Marlie?"

"Maybe not about how he felt, but he sure complained about everything else," Marla Jo replied.

"So, are you saying he didn't complain about feeling ill?" Donovan asked.

"No, he didn't. Not really. But, he did miss quite a bit of work. He just wouldn't say why. He'd just stay home and watch TV. I don't think he ever saw a doctor." She hesitated. "He lost a lot of weight, though. And, his appetite wasn't what it used to be."

"Did he still do a lot of drinking?"

"Probably more. Even if he missed work, he would still be at Kelsey's every night. The alcohol probably killed any pain he might have been having. But, Frank liked his liquor and I don't think anything would have stopped him from drinking."

"His appetite seemed pretty good the day he died,"

Donovan commented. "Plus, he seemed in a pretty good mood when we got here."

"He'd been drinking," Betsy said. "He'd spent a few hours at Kelsey's that day."

Donovan looked surprised. "He drank that early in the day?"

"Not every day, but it was his birthday and he started celebrating early," Betsy told him.

Marla Jo picked up a cookie and bit into it. "What are you getting at, Donovan?

Donovan looked at the plate of cookies. "Those look good. What kind are they?"

"What difference does it make? Have one. My mother makes the best cookies in the world. And, I can guarantee you, Donovan, that they are 100% poop-free."

"Marla Jo!" Betsy yelled. "That is not even a little bit funny."

27

"Jimmy Knowles?" Donovan asked the man behind the bar.

"The one and only," Knowles replied. "What can I do you for?" he inquired, smiling.

"I'm Detective Donovan from the 3rd Precinct. I wonder if you could spare a few minutes? I'd like to ask you a few questions."

Knowles looked around at the empty room and grinned. "I think I can break away for a few minutes. Can I get you anything?"

"Coffee would be great." Donovan turned to Detective Fritz. "You want some coffee?"

"I could go for a cup," Fritz replied.

Knowles grabbed a couple of coffee cups, poured the coffee, and placed them on the bar in front of the cops. "I imagine this is about Frank McKnight. I wondered when one of you guys would show up."

Donovan took a sip of the hot coffee and smiled. "Try it, Fritz. This is a hell of a cup of coffee."

Knowles grinned. "It's the best coffee in town."

"Knowles, I talked to Betsy McKnight last night and I'd like to follow up on a few things we talked about."

"How is Betsy? " Knowles asked.

"She seems to be doing okay, considering the circumstances," Donovan told him.

"Yeah. Real shame about Frank," Knowles said, obviously holding back a grin.

"You don't seem too broke up about it," Fritz observed.

"I'm not. He was a real prick. So, what do you want

to know?" Knowles asked.

"I understand you and Betsy dated in high school, kind of lost touch after you went into the service, and then reconnected a few years back. Is that right?"

"Sounds about right. After I opened the bar and grill, she and Frank were here a lot. Especially Frank. He did like his spirits."

"How often did Betsy come in?"

Knowles shrugged. "At first, she came in a lot with Frank but - well, not so much lately. Frank didn't want her coming here after my wife died. I think he had some harebrained idea that I was going to make a play for her. Anyway, I was kinda glad she stopped coming in as often as she used to."

"Really?" Donovan asked. "Why's that?"

"I couldn't stand to watch the way he treated her. He was always cussing her out about something. I'm pretty sure he hit her. A lot. She always had a few bruises. I asked her about it one time, but she wouldn't talk about it. God, I can't stand a man who hits a woman."

"Did you ever see him hit her?" Donovan inquired.

"I saw him come close one time to almost hitting her. I was about to go over the bar to try to stop him but one of my customers stepped up and grabbed his arm before he made contact. He would do other things, though. Like grab her arm and squeeze it or push her away. He was a real bastard, that's for sure," Knowles exclaimed. "I can't say I'm sorry he's dead."

"If you didn't like the guy, why'd you let him keep coming here? Why not just tell him to go elsewhere?"

"You gotta understand, Detective, that this is a neighborhood bar. My customers have been coming here for years. We're like a big family. Families usually have that one black sheep that no one really cares for but tolerates. I guess that was Frank. He was an okay guy until he got a little too much booze in him. But, after a few, he could get downright nasty. I sat him down and talked to him after the fight and he seemed to settle down a bit. I threatened to cut him off if he didn't cool it. And, he had a three-drink limit. How about that?

"How did he handle that? Only being allowed three drinks, I mean?" Donovan asked him.

"At first he would argue after the third drink. He wanted me to serve him more. But, when he found out I was serious, he seemed to accept it. The truth is though. . ."

"What?" Donovan prompted.

"Well, I think he usually had a few before he got here. I can't say for sure, but he acted like it. I let it slide because he always walked here. He only lived a few blocks away, you know. If he had been driving, it would have been a different story."

"Did you notice anything different about him after the fight? Did he seem ill? Betsy said he lost a lot of weight. Did he ever mention feeling ill?"

"Yeah, I seem to recall that he did. A couple of times he complained about having stomach pains, feeling tired, and some G.I. problems. I just figured it was the booze catching up with him."

"Tell me about the night of the fight. I know it was between Frank and Richard Stiverson and a guy called Percy. What's Percy's last name?"

"Fritz. The same as your detective friend here. Percy Fritz." He looked at Detective Fritz. "Any relation?"

"Not that I'm aware of," Fritz told him.

"Anyway, Percy wasn't fighting. It was Frank and Richie. Percy was trying to break it up. Man, those two tore this place up real good."

"Excuse me," Detective Fritz interrupted. "What was the fight about, anyway?"

"You don't know?" Knowles asked, surprised.

"Haven't quite got to that yet," Donovan told him.

"It started after Richie stepped in and stopped Frank from hitting Betsy. After Richie grabbed Frank's arm, Frank went ballistic. I got Betsy out of the way, called the cops, and let them go at it. To tell you the truth, I was hoping that Richie would beat the crap out of Frank. Percy – who is a really big guy, by the way – managed to break it up before the cops got here."

"Betsy was here?"

"She sure was."

"You didn't know she was here?" Fritz asked Donovan.

"Not a clue. She never mentioned it."

"Can I top off your coffee?" Knowles asked.

"I'm good," Detective Fritz said.

"I'll take a little more," Donovan told him and watched as Knowles emptied the pot into his cup. "Tell me, Jimmy, do you think any of your customers hated Frank enough to want him dead?"

Knowles snorted. "Are you serious? It would be a lot shorter list if I wrote down any of them that didn't."

"That bad, huh?"

"Yep. I'd say so," Knowles replied.

"Who are your top three?"

"I don't know if I want to play this game, Detective Donovan."

"I'm not playing. Name them."

"Shit." Knowles thought for a moment. "Well, Richie, of course." He hesitated. "John Meyer and Frank fought a lot. Mostly about politics and shit and they would get into it pretty good. It never came to blows, though." He shrugged.

"Where does Meyer live?" Detective Fritz asked.

"He lived a few blocks over on Madison Street."

"Lived? Did he move?" Fritz asked.

"Nope. He died. Heart attack, it was. Gone in a matter of minutes. That's how I want to go. Fast, like that."

"Help me out here, Jimmy. Give me one more name."

Knowles frowned. "Me. I guess I'd be in the top three. I hated that son of a bitch. I hated the way he treated Betsy. She deserved a lot better than him. Yeah, I guess I'd be on that list, too."

"So, did you?"

"Did I what?"

"Kill him? Was it you?"

"I understand you were sitting at the table when he died, Detective Donovan. Did you see me there?" Knowles replied, grinning.

"Good point," Donovan replied smiling. "Did you ever see anyone put anything in Frank's drink?"

Knowles laughed. "Even if I had, I sure as hell wouldn't tell you. If someone murdered Frank they did us all a favor. Sorry, Detective, I can't help you."

Donovan looked down at his cell phone and frowned when he read the text. "Sorry," he told the two men. "I've got to take this." He stepped away from the bar and walked over to the window. He hit a number on speed dial and waited.

"Hi."

"What's so important? I'm working here, M. J."

"They dug up dad last night, Donovan. The coroner we are using isn't quite done yet, but he has found something interesting that 'your' medical examiner seems to have missed and it's important. I thought you'd like to know."

Donovan's stomach fluttered as he prepared himself for another piece of bad news.

"Donovan?"

"Let me have it," Donovan said.

"Dad was poisoned. It seems. . ."

"That's it?" Donovan exclaimed. "We already know that there was poison in his system, M. J."

"Let me finish!" she yelled. "God, you're so.... I don't know. Impatient. That's it. You're so fricking impatient."

"Sorry," Donovan said.

"Strychnine, Donovan. It was friggin' strychnine. And, I'll tell you right now before you even think about saying it. It was not my mother!"

"I wasn't going to say that," Donovan protested.

"You weren't?"

"No. Because I have a very good idea who it might have been."

"You do?" Marla Jo asked.

"Yes. And, to put your mind at ease, it wasn't anyone in your family. Thanks for calling. I'll get back to you," Donovan said and cut off the call. "She's not the only one who doesn't have to say goodbye," he muttered to himself.

"Fritz," he called out. "Something has come up. We've got to go." He turned to Knowles and smiled. "Thanks for your help, Jimmy."

"Hey, no problemo. Glad I could help."

Detective Fritz shut the car door and looked at Donovan. "Whataya got?"

"It looks like Frank McKnight was poisoned all right. Only, it wasn't any damn berries or dog poop. It looks like it was strychnine."

"No shit!" Fritz exclaimed.

"We need to get to a judge and get a search warrant."

"For the McKnight house?"

"Nope. For Kelsey's Bar and Grill."

28

"Hey, Donovan, I was just going to call you," Officer Chesterton remarked as Donovan walked into the squad room.

"What's up?"

"Willy Richards from the 8th Precinct called. They gotta match on those prints from the Stiverson house."

"No shit. Who is it?"

"Some guy called Sam Heller. Have you ever heard of him?"

"Heller? His name doesn't sound familiar. What's his story?"

"Not much to tell. Nothing violent. He's been picked up a few times for shoplifting. Nothing big. Just food. He never served any time, though."

"Grocery stores?"

"Yup. All different stores and none of the managers wanted to press charges. They felt sorry for the guy. Richards is out looking for him right now. He said he'd give you a call later. What have you been up to?"

Donovan grinned. "We may just have Frank McKnight's killer. I'm waiting on Fritz to get a judge to sign a search warrant."

"Who is it this time?" Chesterton asked grinning. "The spinster aunt?"

"Real funny. And, no. It's not anyone in the family. It looks like the owner of Kelsey's Bar and Grill may have been involved. Or, Stiverson. It could be him."

"Wait a minute, Donovan. Aren't you getting your cases confused? How could Stiverson be one of them or is it a different Stiverson?"

"The same one. It's kinda complicated. I'm positive that someone at Kelsey's was putting strychnine in McKnight's drinks. The logical person is Jimmy Knowles, the owner of the bar. But, a lot of his customers hated McKnight and could have done it. And that includes Stiverson who is a regular there. But, right now, my money is on Knowles. I think he has a thing for Frank's wife, Betsy."

Officer Chesterton sat back in his chair, looking confused. "Say what?"

"I said it was complicated."

"So, Stiverson is a suspect in both the cases you're working on. That's not something you see very often."

"I don't like Stiverson as a person. He's a real son of a bitch. But, I've eliminated him as a suspect in Barbara Stiverson's death. I believe he was fishing when she was killed."

"However, you think he could be involved in McKnight's death?"

"They had history. McKnight wasn't liked and he and Stiverson went a few rounds a while back. He could have slipped something into McKnight's drinks. They both spent a lot of time there."

Chesterton looked over at the door. "Fritz is here."

Donovan glanced over at the door as Fritz walked in holding up a piece of paper. "Got it," he yelled, grinning. "Let's go."

"You wanna come, Chesterton?"

"Hell, yes. I love search warrants. Do you need anyone else?"

"Yeah. Grab Bailey and Peterson and let's go."

An hour later, Donovan set a box of rat poison, that

had been bagged and tagged, on the table in front of Knowles. "Do you care to explain what you're doing with this?"

Knowles pushed it away. "Just why are you searching my bar, Detective?"

"I think you killed Frank McKnight. And, I think this is the poison you used to do it."

Knowles looked at him and shook his head. "You are so far off base. I'll bet you a hundred bucks that you will find rat poison in every bar and restaurant in town. We all have those filthy vermin now and then and this is the best way to get rid of them. For God's sake, I didn't kill Frank. I may not have liked the man, but I sure as hell didn't kill him."

"How long have you been seeing Betsy McKnight?"

Knowles's head jerked up and he stared at Donovan. "Who told you?" he finally asked.

Donovan grinned. "So, it's true. Just answer the question. How long has it been going on?"

"We've gone out a few times since Frank died."

"Were you fooling around while Frank was still alive?"

"Hell, no!" Knowles exclaimed. "Betsy is a lady and she would never do anything like that. Be careful how you talk about her, Donovan."

"Frank hasn't been gone that long and she's already dating? Seems kind of quick to me."

"We're old friends. I told you I've known her since high school. We go out for dinner once in a while. That's all there is to it."

"Well, Jimmy, I'm gonna have to take you in. Right now you're my number one suspect in Frank's murder. And, unless you can show me I'm wrong. . . Well, you're looking pretty good for it as far as I'm concerned."

"You're wrong."

"Then prove it. Give me something."

"Well, for one thing, I wasn't working the morning that Frank died. If someone put a little rat poison in his drink that day, it wasn't me."

"Yeah, well who was working that morning?"

"Stiverson."

"Really? He works here?"

"He occasionally fills in when I need someone. He runs a tab here and, well. . ."

"Okay, I get it. He works to pay down his tab." Donovan interrupted. "Tell me, Jimmy, are we gonna find his prints on that box of poison?

"I don't think so. I can't think of any reason that Stiverson would have put poison out. It certainly isn't part of his job description."

"Isn't it against the health rules to be putting poison out around food? It doesn't seem right to me," Donovan inquired.

"I use metal traps and put the poison inside. The traps are never out in the open. The rats go inside the trap, the trap closes, the rats eat the poison and they die. It seems a little more humane to me."

"Killing them by breaking their little necks or by poisoning them – well, none of it seems humane to me. But, whatever works, I guess."

"Darn tooting," Knowles said, grinning.

"Excuse me for a minute. I'll be right back," Donovan said and walked out of the bar, took out his phone, and made a call.

"Hi, this is Detective Donovan of the 3rd Precinct," he told the person who answered the phone. "I'd like to speak to District Attorney Autry." He waited a few moments for the D.A. to come on the phone. "Dale, Bobby Donovan here. I have a. . ."

"Bobby, long time no hear. How are you?" D.A. Autry interrupted.

"Fine, thanks. Listen, I have a legal question I was hoping you could answer for me."

"What's that, Bobby?"

"Let's say a man kills another man. Then, in a totally unrelated crime, a woman is murdered and this man is innocent of that crime. The murdered woman had two insurance policies and this man – who is the beneficiary of these policies - will collect one and a half million dollars when the insurance pays him. If he is found guilty of murdering the man, is he still entitled to the money?"

"Can you repeat that?" Dale said laughing.

"I'd rather not."

"That's all right. I think I got it. So this man is a suspect in a murder that you're working on?"

"Right."

"And, he's also a beneficiary of an insurance policy in a different case you're working on?

"Right."

"And, the woman who owned the policy was murdered?"

"Right."

"And, you want to know if he is convicted of killing the man, can he still collect from the woman's estate? And, the two crimes are not related? Do I have it?"

"Sounds complicated, doesn't it?" Donovan asked.

"I don't know," Autry told him.

"What do you mean, you don't know?"

"Exactly what I said. I don't know. I think it's up to the insurance company. I think you should check with them."

"That's all you got?" Donovan asked.

"Sorry. My gut instinct is that the man would be entitled to the money seeing as one case has nothing to do with the other. But, again, I suggest you check with the insurance company."

Donovan sighed. "I'll do that. Thanks, anyway, Dale."

"Always good to talk to you, Bobby. Sorry I couldn't help."

Donovan ended the call. He watched the traffic go by for a few moments before he called Marla Jo. "I'd like to speak to Ms. McKnight, please," he said when a man answered the phone.

"May I ask who is calling?"

"Tell her it's Detective Donovan."

"One moment, please."

"Donovan, what's up?" Marla Jo said as she answered his call.

"I need to know something. . ."

"I'm mad at you, you know."

Donovan rolled his eyes. "I'm sorry I hung up on you."

"It's very rude, you know."

"I know. And, it's rude when you do it to me, too," he responded.

"I don't do that," Marla Jo protested.

"Ah, but you do. Now, can we get back to business?"

"We have business?"

"Stop it, M. J. I'm busy here and I need to know something."

"The answer is yes," she declared.

"What's yes?"

"Yes, you're good in bed. Is there anything else you need to know?"

Donovan took a deep breath and let it out. "Are you done?"

"Sorry. I guess your sense of humor is taking a break today. What do you need?"

"Who answered the phone?"

"That's why you called?"

"Of course not. I was just wondering where Ida is?"

"She's gone. I've hired someone."

"A man?"

"Men can be secretaries. He's very good. So, what can I do to help you?"

"It's about Stiverson. If he killed your dad can he still get the money from the insurance policies?"

"You think he killed my dad?"

"There's a possibility."

Marla Jo didn't say anything.

"Are you still there?" Donovan asked.

"They are unrelated cases, so I'd say the answer is yes. However, I'm going to check with one of our attorneys to be sure. Can I get back to you?"

"Of course." Donovan hesitated. "Do you really think so?"

"What? That it's a possibility he can collect?"

"No. That I'm good in bed." He waited. "M. J.? Are you still there?"

29

"Where did you say you were?"

"I'm in my car. I've got to get out of town. I got word that the cops are looking for me. I need the rest of my money."

"I told you before, Sam, I don't have it."

"Now you listen, you fucking asshole. You owe me ninety-five hundred dollars and I want it. Charlie and I need to get someplace safe."

"The best I can do is a couple hundred."

"No fucking way!" Sam screamed into the phone. "You have an hour. One hour! That's it!"

"Sorry, old friend. I can't do it."

Sam took a deep breath and let it out. He knew it was only a matter of time before the cops would be pounding on his door. "This is the last time I'm asking. If I go down, you're going with me. Understand?"

"I got it. You need money. And, what you need to understand is that I'm broke, Sam. I'm not getting any insurance payout. I'm in real trouble."

"Well, boohoo. You'll be in a lot more trouble if you don't get me my money."

"All right. Let me think a minute. It's hard to think with you yelling at me."

Sam waited a few moments. "Well?" he yelled.

"I've got a CD I can cash in. I'll only get about sixty-five hundred, though. That's the best I can do."

"Then, do it. I'll meet you in an hour."

"Sam, the bank isn't open yet. Can you give me a little more time?" He waited for Sam's answer. "Sam?"

"I'm sorry. Did you say you wanted more time?" Sam

asked him.

"All right. Just forget it. An hour, it is."

"Same place, then? Under the overpass?"

"Yeah. In the meantime, don't get caught for, God's sake."

"Just make sure you show up with the money or there will be hell to pay."

"Don't worry. I'll be there. And, Sam?"

"What?"

"After this, I never want to hear from you again. Got it?"

"Got it. One hour."

<u>30</u>

"Hey, Willy, what's happening?" Donovan asked when Detective Richards answered the phone.

"Morning, Bobby."

"Good news, hey? I understand our guy is Sam Heller. Have you picked him up yet?"

"Nah, we just got his address. I'll be sending a few guys over to his house this morning to bring him in. You want in when I interview him?"

"Hell, yes, I want in. His prints are all over a murder victim's house. I certainly want to know what he was doing there."

"You mean besides stealing food? That's his thing, you know. Stealing food," Richards declared.

"Yeah, well cutting up bodies may be his thing, too."

"You still think he's good for that murder?"

"I think he was there, at least. I'm not sure he murdered her but I think he probably helped chop her up," Donovan replied.

"I don't know. There's nothing violent in his history, Bobby. I'm pretty sure he took the food from her house, but that could have been done at any time. His prints could have been in that house for weeks before the murder."

"You might be right, but my gut is telling me that he had something to do with her murder. Anyway, we'll find out."

"That was a hell of a game last night, wasn't it?"

"I didn't watch it. Busy, you know."

"Too busy to watch one of the best games. . ." Richards stopped talking and laughed. "You devil. Good for you."

"I gotta go, Willy. Give me a call when you get the guy, okay?" Donovan asked.

"Will do, you devil you."

At exactly 9:30 a.m., Sam Heller drove his car under the overpass and shut it off. He turned and looked behind him. "You okay back there, Charlie?" he asked. He watched as a car pulled up beside him. "He better have it all," he told Charlie as he rolled down his car window.

"Sam, I've got it," the man yelled as he held up a paper bag. He opened his car door and got out. As he walked over to Sam's car, he held out the bag and yelled, "You wanna see it?"

"Hell, yes, I want to see it. And, I wanna count it, too."

"No problem. It's all there."

As Sam reached for it, the man put his hand inside the bag and pulled out a gun. "You idiot. You didn't really think I'd give you the money, did you?" he asked grinning.

"What do you think you're doing?" Sam yelled when he saw the gun.

"You know what, Sam? You're like a pimple on my ass that won't go away." He pointed the gun at Sam's face. "Goodbye, Sam."

"No! For God's sake, don't! Charlie needs me."

"Oh, don't you worry about Charlie. I'll take good care of him," the man said as he pulled the trigger, shooting Sam between the eyes, killing him instantly. He opened the back door and looked at Charlie, who was laying on the back seat, staring at him. "What about you, old boy?

Charlie whimpered softly and looked away.

"Sorry, old boy," he uttered, pulled the trigger, and walked back to his car.

"Hey, Donovan," Officer Chesterton called across the squad room. "There's a call for you. It's Willy Richards."

Donovan picked up the phone. "Willy, I didn't expect to hear from you so soon. You got Heller?"

"Oh, we got him all right. He's dead."

"What the hell happened? Did he go down fighting?" Donovan inquired.

"Nah, nothing like that. He was found in his car, shot right between the eyes. It looks like someone didn't want him talking."

"When did it happen?"

"The body is fresh. The coroner says he was killed a few hours ago."

"It looks like we just can't get a break."

"I'm not sure about that, Bobby. We got some prints off the car. Most of them are Heller's, of course, but there were a few others that we're checking out now."

"Well, maybe we'll get lucky. However, the way this case is going, I doubt it."

"We found a dog in the back seat of his car, Donovan."

"A dog?"

"Yeah. Dead. The asshole shot the dog, too. He looked like he was pretty old. Hell, he had more gray hair than I do. He probably would have died before long anyway but the prick didn't have to kill him."

"Rotten son of a bitch."

"You're right. Anyway, according to his tags, the dog's name was Charlie.

"Ah, crap, Richards."

"What?" Richards asked.

"Think about it. Heller was stealing food to feed his dog and himself. Dogs love raw meat. You know, like. . ."

"Toes?" Richards interrupted. "Man, that's just sick."

"You think? But, I guess, to a dog, food is just food, no matter where it came from. Have you any idea what type of gun was used?"

"A .45, we think. The coroner will tell us for sure."

"Are your guys searching his house?"

"CSI is there right now," Richards told Donovan. "Hopefully, we will find something that ties him to the Stiverson murder."

"Well, we already know he was in the house."

"But, that doesn't prove he was there when the murder took place."

"I know," Donovan said. "Just find something, will you? I'm positive it was Freemont who killed her. I just can't prove it."

"We'll do our best, Bobby."

"I know. Call me when you have more information."

"Will do."

Marla Jo looked up from her desk and smiled. "Yes, Marcus?"

"I'm going to lunch. Can I bring you anything?" he asked.

"I'm going out for lunch, but thanks for asking."

"Are you going with that Detective Donovan?" he asked, grinning.

"Well, now, I don't know if that's any of your business," she replied.

"I'm sorry. That was out of line. Please don't fire me," he begged, laughing at his remark.

"Not a chance. It will take more than that for me to get rid of you. Enjoy your lunch."

Marcus stared at her for a few seconds. "Thanks. You, too," he said, walking out of Marla Jo's office.

Marla Jo sighed, wondering how much longer she would last before she kicked his sweet butt out. His incessant talking and stupid jokes were driving her crazy. Oh, well, she thought, he was still better than Ida. She grabbed her purse and headed out to meet Donovan for lunch.

"They killed the dog?" she exclaimed. "Dear God, Donovan, what kind of person would do that? Oh, that poor poor dog."

Donovan sat back in his chair and stared at Marla Jo. "What about the man?"

"The man made his choices. He probably had it coming. The dog didn't do anything wrong."

"Well, he probably ate some parts of Barbara Stiverson. That's certainly not right."

"He was a dog. And, probably hungry. Dogs don't know any different, Donovan. I don't feel sorry for that Heller guy. I feel sorry for the dog."

Donovan shook his head. "You are a strange one, M. J."

"I guarantee you that ninety-nine people out of a hundred would feel sorry for the dog – and only the dog."

"You've convicted the man before he has been found guilty, you know."

Marla Jo thought for a few moments. "You may be right. Anyway, the way the world is today, people like pets more than people."

Donovan took a bite of his sandwich and shook his head. "I think you may be right."

"You really shouldn't talk with your mouth full. It isn't pleasant to watch."

He glared at her for a second and then swallowed his food. "And, you should quit hanging up on me."

Marla Jo laughed. "Touché."

"I'm waiting to see whose prints are on the box of rat poison we took from Kelseys Bar. If Stiverson's show up, I'm going to arrest him for your father's murder," Donovan said and took another bite of his sandwich.

Marla Jo looked surprised for a moment and, then, smiled. "That's good news, Donovan. Are you positive he did it, though?"

"For God's sake, M. J. Do you think I would arrest someone just because I didn't like them? If it wasn't him, then I'm going to have to go with Jimmy Knowles."

"I doubt Jimmy did it. He wouldn't do that to my mother. He would know it would hurt her."

"Maybe. Or, he might have been doing her a favor. He knew how your dad was with her."

"I know." Marla Jo sighed. "Well, it won't make any difference as far as The Second Century is concerned. He is still entitled to collect the insurance."

"You checked with the attorneys?"

"I did. They will try to fight it if he did kill dad. Or, make him an offer to avoid a trial, but there's a ninety-five percent chance that Stiverson will get it. Are you sure he didn't kill Barbara Stiverson?"

"We are. At least right now we are pretty sure it was Freemont."

"But, you can't prove it. Can you?" Marla Jo asked.

"I'm hoping the search of Heller's house will give us something."

"When will you know?"

"I'm waiting for Detective Richards to call."

"I'll give you unlimited back rubs and sex for a month if you arrest Stiverson for her murder. Couldn't you plant some evidence against him?"

Donovan laughed. "You're bribing me with back rubs and sex? You definitely are a company person, aren't you?"

"Does that mean no?"

"I'm afraid it does," Donovan replied grinning.

"That's a shame. It could have been fun. Well, I've got to be getting back to work. Thanks for lunch, Donovan."

"How about dinner tonight at your place? I can bring some take-out."

Marla Jo smiled. "Sounds good, but make it something spicy, will ya? It seems I'm in the mood for something hot."

Donovan grinned. "Hot is good. I can do hot. And, maybe I'll talk you into one of those back rubs."

31

"I'm giving you the Heller case," Richards told Donovan.

"You're doing what? Why in the world would you do that?"

"Well, I figure I owe you one, Bobby. You helped us out a while back with the Marchetti case. We never would have solved that one if it wasn't for you. All we have on Heller is a few robberies."

"That's true, but giving up a murder case. . . Well, that's big, man."

"Like I said, I owe ya."

"I'll take it. Thanks, Willy."

"Are you sitting down, 'cause now you're really gonna love me? I've got the results of the prints they pulled off Heller's car."

"You found a match?"

"We sure did. It was one that we took off of the back door handle. Oh, man, you're gonna love me for this one."

Donovan waited. "Well?" he finally asked. "Who do they belong to?"

"Mr. Alfred Freemont."

"I fucking knew it," Donovan yelled. "Does he own a gun? Did you check yet?"

"We're running that now to see if he's a registered owner. Anyway, I'm turning it all over to you. I'll drop off everything we have so far later this afternoon. Maybe, we can go get a beer or something."

"How's your boss with that, Willy? Giving everything to us here at the 3rd, I mean? That's a pretty big deal."

"Bobby, we are so backed up here – well, you just

wouldn't believe it." He paused for a second. "Actually, it was his idea."

Donovan laughed. "So much for owing me one."

"Hey, I could have said no to him. I figure we're even."

"I guess. Anyway, I appreciate it."

"And, Bobby?"

"Yeah?"

"We found Heller's phone in the car. You might want to check it out. You know, check his texts and calls and stuff to see who he'd been talking to. I'm bringing it with me."

"Absolutely. Hopefully, there are calls on it to Freemont."

"It would help. Anywho, I'm super busy and I've got to go. I'll see you around five. Maybe we can get a burger with that beer. You got any places around there that makes a good burger?"

"They all do. Thanks, Willy. See ya."

Donovan hung up the phone and fist-bumped the air. "Yes!" he yelled.

Detective Fritz glanced over at him and grinned. "I take it you got good news."

"It looks like we got Freemont."

"For who? Stiverson or Heller?" Fritz asked.

Donovan stared at him. "Heller," he said after a few moments. "Shit. Right now all I can connect him to for sure is Heller's murder."

"Did I hear right? Richards is turning the Heller case over to you?"

Donovan shook his head yes. "He's dropping off all the stuff later."

Fritz grinned. "Do you think maybe you bit off a little more than you can chew, Donovan?"

"Not really, if you think about it. I'll have it all contained here now. I don't have to be going back and forth with Richards. I know Freemont did Heller in. I know Heller was in the Stiverson house. They knew each other, that's for sure. It's only a matter of putting the pieces together."

"Good luck," Fritz told him.

Donovan thought for a few seconds, picked up the phone, and called Marla Jo.

"How come you're calling on my cell?" she asked as she picked up her phone.

"It's easier than going through your secretary. And, hello to you, too."

"Sorry. Hello, Donovan. What's up?"

"I'm not going to be able to make it tonight. We got a break in the Barbara Stiverson case. Anyway, I'm meeting Detective Richards from the 8th Precinct to go over the evidence he's collected so far. He's turning everything over to me."

"I don't understand," Marla Jo commented. "I didn't know he was working on the Stiverson case."

"He isn't," Donovan told her. "He's been working on the Heller case and so have we. I should have said that he's handing the Heller case over to me. It's better that way."

"And, that gives you a break in the Stiverson case how?"

"We figure the Heller case and the Stiverson case are intermingled. Once we get the Heller case figured out, I'm pretty sure we'll be able to close the Stiverson case. I know it's confusing, M. J., but I think Heller helped

Freemont kill Barbara Stiverson. Anyway, I'm sorry I can't make it tonight."

"I understand. You do know what you will be missing, don't you?"

"Come on, M. J., don't play dirty."

"What dirty? I'm talking about that hot spicy food. Get your mind out of the gutter, Donovan."

"Yeah, right. That's what you were talking. . . Are you still there?" He looked at his phone and shook his head. "I don't believe this woman," he mumbled.

Fritz looked over at Donovan, "What's that? Did you say something?"

32

At ten-thirty the next morning, Donovan received a phone call verifying that there were phone calls and text messages made to Alfred Freemont from Sam Heller's phone. After asking the IT guy numerous questions regarding the calls and texts, he was informed that calls had been made between the two men before and shortly after Barbara Stiverson was murdered. There were also a few calls made by Heller to Freemont during the weeks following Stiverson's death. Donovan determined that he had enough information to arrest Freemont

It was interesting, Donovan thought, that Freemont made no calls to Heller after Stiverson was killed. All the calls between the two of them were instigated by Heller. But, best of all, the phone records showed that Heller called Freemont the morning of his murder.

Figuring he had enough evidence to issue a search warrant of Freemont's car and house, he placed a call to District Attorney Dale Autry.

"Bobby, I didn't expect to hear from you again so soon."

"Morning, Dale. How are you?"

"Fine. I hope the same can be said for you. What can I do for you now?"

"I need another search warrant. This one is for Alfred Freemont's house and car. We will be arresting him shortly for the murder of one Samuel Heller and his dog, Charlie. We'd like to serve the search warrant when we go to pick him up."

"He killed a dog?"

"I'm afraid so. And, right now, he's also looking good

for the murder of Barbara Stiverson. However, we're still working on gathering evidence on that case."

"How did he kill him?" Dale asked.

"Shot him right between his eyes. I gather they had a falling out and Heller was about to spill the beans."

"No, how did he kill the dog?"

Donovan looked up at the ceiling and rolled his eyes. He let out a big sigh and told her, "He shot him between the eyes, too."

"Damn. I hate to hear that."

"Yeah, it's a shame. So, can I send one of my men to pick up the warrant?"

"I'll have it ready for him if there's a judge around to sign it. How did the last warrant you asked for work out? Did you get your man?"

"I'm not sure. We're still processing everything."

"Well, good luck," the district attorney said.

"I'm sending Officer Chesterton to pick up the warrant. And, thanks a ton, Dale."

"Absolutely. No problem. Do you have any pets, Bobby?"

"No. I've always thought about getting a dog, but I work so much that I figure it wouldn't be fair to the animal.

"Then, get a cat. They are so independent that they practically take care of themselves."

"Is that right? Well, I'll have to think about that. Thanks again, Dale."

"Sure thing. Bye, now."

Donovan hung up the phone and stared at the light above his desk. Suddenly he looked away. "Damn, that's bright," he uttered, trying to blink away the spots before his eyes. "Fritz," he called out.

"Yo," Fritz replied.

"We're gonna go pick up Freemont. Grab a couple of uniforms to go with us."

"Got it," Fritz said.

Donovan looked at Chesterton. "I want you to go over to the D.A.'s office and pick up a search warrant. She'll have it ready for you."

"Now?" Chesterton asked.

"Yes, now. Go get it and meet us at Freemont's house."

Fritz stood up, grinning. "So, we're finally gonna bring that s.o.b. in. Great."

"We got him for Heller, Fritz. And, hopefully, we'll get him for Stiverson before this day is over."

"You might as well settle down," Donovan said. "You're gonna be here for a while."

"I'll have your badge for this, Donovan," Freemont yelled. "What right do you have to treat me like some kind of criminal? I'm gonna sue your ass off."

"You're kidding, right? You are a criminal. You've killed two people that I know about. There could be more for all I know. Oh, yeah, and a dog. Why the hell did you shoot the dog?"

Freemont shot him a dirty look. "I don't know what you're talking about. I didn't kill two people and I certainly didn't kill any dumb dog."

"Yeah, you did. And, you know what? If you hadn't opened that back door of the car to shoot that dumb dog – as you called him – we never would have found your fingerprints. But, then, you were also dumb enough to leave Heller's phone in his car so we could check out his calls and texts. Thanks. I appreciate that."

"It couldn't be my fingerprints, because I never touched any car door and I don't know anyone named Heller."

Donovan sat back in his chair and shook his head. "Oh, you poor deluded man. Did you really think you'd get away with killing him? You should have just given Heller the money and you'd be sitting in your big house without a care in the world. But, it's kinda like dominos, you know. When one falls, it brings them all down."

Freemont looked away and coughed. "I'm not feeling well. I need to see a doctor."

"Of course. We'll get you one just as soon as we're done talking here. Would you care for some water?"

"Please," Freemont replied, coughing again.

Donovan turned to Chesterton and smiled. "Would you get Mr. Freemont some water?"

Chesterton stood up and walked towards the door. "Do you want anything, Detective Donovan?"

"I'm good. I still have some coffee here." He held up his hand. "Oh, wait," he said. "Would you also bring in a copy of the letter that we found in Mr. Heller's house? You know the one I mean, don't you? It's the one where he confesses everything that happened to Mrs. Stiverson."

Freemont's head jerked up in surprise. "What the hell are you talking about?"

"You really shouldn't have killed Heller, Alfred. The only thing that his letter doesn't tell us is how you two knew each other."

"He left a letter?" Freemont yelled. "That idiot left a letter?"

"He did and I wouldn't call him an idiot. I think he was pretty smart putting it all down on paper in case something happened to him."

"Well, then, if he wrote it all down," Freemont shouted sarcastically, "you know I didn't kill Barbara."

"That may be. However, you helped chop her up. That had to be a lot of work. No wonder you hired Heller to help you."

"I didn't do anything, really," Freemont said. "Mary killed her and Sam cut her into all those pieces. I mostly just watched Sam. Barbara was already dead when we got to the house."

"However, you definitely planned it and that will add a few more years to your sentence. Hell, you're already an old man. You won't be spending a lot of time in prison. Why didn't you just pay him? All this would have been avoided if you'd lived up to your agreement."

"Because I'm almost broke. But you know that, don't you?" Freemont coughed again. "Can I have that water?"

Donovan looked at Chesterton, who was still standing at the door listening to the conversation. "Go on. Get him a bottle of water."

"What about Mary?" Freemont asked. "What's gonna happen to her?"

"Ah, Mary Johanson. Our murderess. She's in the other room spilling her guts to Detective Fritz. Although, she may get a break if she testifies against you."

Freemont took a deep breath and coughed again. "I think I need an attorney," he said."

"That's probably a good idea, Alfred," Donovan said grinning.

"Take these cuffs off me, will you? I'm serious, Donovan. I'm not feeling well."

"I wouldn't be feeling well either if I was you."

"I mean it, you asshole. My chest hurts and I. . ."

Freemont grabbed his arm. "Oh, God, I think I'm having a heart attack," he mumbled.

Donovan watched him as he slouched down in the chair and his head fell forward. "Oh, shit!" he yelled. He ran to the door and shouted, "Call 911. We've got an emergency in here."

33

"You look nice," Donovan commented.

"So do you," Marla Jo told him.

"Thanks for meeting me. It's been a long day and I didn't feel like driving all the way to your office."

"No problem."

"I'm afraid I have some bad news," Donovan said, as they slid into a booth.

Marla Jo frowned. "I had a feeling. What's up, Donovan?"

"Alfred Freemont confessed to killing Barbara Stiverson. I'm afraid your company is going to have to pay Richard Stiverson his money."

"I kinda figured that might happen," Marla Jo replied. "Well, at least you've solved your case."

"Alfred Freemont is dead," Donovan announced as he picked up his menu and glanced at it.

"What did you just say?" Marla Jo asked, looking shocked. "He's dead? What happened?"

"Dropped dead of a heart attack while I was interrogating him."

Marla Jo stared at him. "What did you do? Scare him to death?"

"Funny."

"I thought so."

"No, I didn't scare him to death. Before he died, he confessed to killing Sam Heller so we have him for that. Once he found out that we had the evidence to convict him of killing Barbara, he just kind of started talking, telling me who did what and how. Sam Heller did most of the dismantling of the body. And, here's something that will blow your mind. Ready?"

Marla Jo stared at him, not answering.

Donovan waited. "All right. Here is it," he said after a few seconds. "Mary Johanson is the one who actually killed her. Stuck her with a needle filled with enough potassium chloride to kill a horse. That sweet lady was hoping she'd get her money just like everyone else. Man, she sure put on a show, didn't she?" He sat back and stared at Marla Jo. "Well?" he said after a few seconds.

"Well, what?"

"Didn't see that coming, did you?"

Marla Jo grinned. "Sure I did. I figured it was her all along."

"You did?" Donovan asked her, looking surprised.

"Of course not," she said, grinning. "I wouldn't have guessed that in a million years. So, she makes sure she's alone in the house with Barbara, sticks her with a needle, and watches her die. Then Freemont comes along and cuts her up - I still don't understand why they had to do that – and all for nothing. Kind of sad isn't it?"

"You missed the part about Sam Heller. He helped Freemont do the slice-and-dice part. Freemont promised him ten thousand dollars plus all the meat and toes he could carry," he said grinning.

"Ugh! That's gross, Donovan, even coming from you."

Donovan laughed. "Anyway, Heller wanted his money, Freemont didn't want to pay him, and so he killed him and Charlie."

"Charlie. That was the dog?"

"Right."

"I forgot his name for a minute. So what's gonna happen to Mary?"

"She'll probably spend the rest of her life behind bars. God, people are so stupid."

"I guess," she said as she glanced at her menu. "I'm starving." Marla Jo glanced at him. "Are you ready to order?"

Donovan watched to be sure that Marla Jo made it safely to her car. Once she drove away, he headed back to the precinct. He had received a text telling him that the fingerprints on the box of poison at Kelsey's had been identified. He didn't want to wait until morning to find out the results.

"What do you mean, Richard Stiverson's prints weren't on the box?" Donovan yelled as he looked at the report.

"What can I tell you, Donovan? If they weren't there they weren't there. What do you want me to do about it?" Fritz replied.

"I know that bastard killed Frank McKnight. My gut is telling me that he poisoned him. I'm as sure as the day is long."

"Yeah, but your gut isn't evidence. You need more than that to go on."

Donovan took a moment to look over the report. "They found three different sets of prints on the box," he commented. "Knowles, of course. That's to be expected. They found some from an ex-con named Alex Hoffman and there were some they couldn't identify."

"You know Donovan, that bar's a busy place. Knowles has got a lot of people working for him. Those prints could have come from anyone."

Donovan sighed. "I guess." He stood up and started

to pace back and forth. "Damn, there's something I can't put my finger on. I'm gonna go talk to Jimmy Knowles again. Do you wanna come with me?"

Fritz shrugged. "I don't know what you think you're gonna find. We searched that whole place."

"You wanna come or not?"

Fritz looked around the squad room. "I wouldn't mind getting some fresh air. Let's go."

"Holy crap," Fritz exclaimed. "This place is packed."

Donovan stood in the doorway, looking for a place to sit.

"There are two at the bar if you want to wait for a table," a waitress told them as she walked by.

"Thanks," Donovan said, still looking around the room.

"Let's go," he told Fritz, as he turned and walked out the door.

Fritz gave him a confused look and followed him. "What's going on?" he asked.

"I need to think a minute," Donovan replied. "The place is packed and this may not be the right time to try to talk to Knowles. It might be better if we come back tomorrow."

"And?" Fritz asked.

Donovan looked at him and let out a deep breath. "Betsy McKnight is in there. I'm not sure I want her to see me."

"I don't get it. What's the difference?"

"She and Knowles go way back. They've known each other since high school."

"So? What's the big deal? Maybe she just wanted something to eat and decided to go where she knows people."

"Yeah, that could be. However, don't you think it would be weird for us to show up here if we weren't working? I'd rather she didn't know what's going on right now."

Fritz studied Donovan's face for a moment. "You think she killed her husband," Fritz stated. "She's on your shortlist, isn't she?"

"Of course, she isn't. . . Well, maybe. Right now I haven't eliminated her."

"Oh, man, you are in so much trouble. You should step off this case."

Donovan frowned. "I know but I can't."

"How serious is it with you and the McKnight woman?"

"I told you. I like her. A lot," Donovan told him.

"Then you better back off. Can you imagine what will happen if you take this any further? You already have half of her family hating you for accusing her nephew of murder. Now you want to take on her mom?"

"I want to prove that her mom didn't have anything to do with it, Fritz. That's all."

"Man, I'm glad I'm not walking in your shoes. You're right. It's best we leave and come back in the morning."

Donovan hesitated a moment. "Yeah. Let's go. Anyway, we should check out that Hoffman guy and find out what's up with him."

"If you keep going after her family. . . What's her name again?"

"Marla Jo."

"If you keep going after Marla Jo's family, you might as well accept the fact that your relationship is over," Fritz told him. "If she finds out what you're doing, she'll kick you to the curb so fast your head will spin."

Donovan looked at him. "Maybe."

"So, this case is more important to you than Marla Jo," Fritz commented.

"I'm not choosing if that's what you're getting at."

"You're an idiot, Donovan. Hand this case over to someone else. Hell, give it to me."

"You know I can't do that, Fritz."

"I know you can't, but you should."

34

Jimmy Knowles looked over at the door, frowned, and continued wiping down the table.

"Morning, Jimmy," Donovan called out. "How are you doing this fine morning?"

Knowles straightened up and forced a smile. "I couldn't be better."

"Morning," Fritz mumbled as he yawned.

"Morning, Detective." He glanced up at Donovan. "I could swear I saw you two in here last night."

"We were. I wanted to talk to you but when I saw how busy you were I changed my mind. You had a hell of a crowd in here last night."

Knowles smiled. "It's like that every night except Monday."

"Why's Monday different?" Fritz asked.

"Because we're closed on Monday." He walked to the next table and started cleaning it. "So, what do you want, Donovan?"

"Do you know Alex Hoffman?"

"Sure. I know Alex. What about it?"

"Where do you know him from?" Donovan asked.

"We were in the Army together. We go way back. When he needs a little extra spending money he works a few nights tending bar or helping in the kitchen."

"Do you know he's an ex-con?"

"Of course, I know that. It was a long time ago."

"Do you usually hire ex-convicts?" Donovan asked.

"I do if they are old friends and I trust them. Alex made a mistake, paid his dues, and he's a stand-up guy. I'd trust him with my life."

"We found his prints on the box of rat poison, Jimmy."

Knowles looked at Donovan and shrugged. "So?"

"So, we want to know why they would be on there. You said you were the only one who baited those traps with that poison. So why are his prints on the box?"

"Are you kidding me? That doesn't mean anything except that he touched the box. Maybe he was trying to kill a few rats. He sure as hell wasn't trying to poison Frank McKnight. You're reaching, Donovan."

"Did they get along?" Donovan asked.

"Who? Frank and Alex? I guess so. At least, as much as anyone got along with Frank. If you're wondering if I think Alex had a reason to kill Frank, the answer is no, I don't."

Donovan glanced over at the bar and spotted the coffee maker. "Is that coffee fresh?" he asked.

Knowles shook his head yes. "Can I get you a cup?"

"If you don't mind."

"Detective Fritz. Would you care for a cup?"

"If it's not too much trouble," Fritz replied.

"Here's the thing, Jimmy," Donovan said, as Knowles walked behind the bar to get the coffee. "I'm pretty positive the poison that killed McKnight came from here. He was being poisoned over a period of time and I'm pretty sure it was someone who worked here or had access to your rat poison. Then, he came in here for a few drinks on the day of his birthday and he was given the fatal dose. It took a few hours to kill him, which is why he died a few hours later during his birthday dinner."

"That might be, but at this point, it's all conjecture on your part," Knowles commented. He set the coffee in front of the two men. "Black, right?"

"Right," Donovan and Fritz said in unison.

"You didn't mention Stiverson," Knowles said. "Did you find his prints on the box of rat poison, too?"

Donovan looked away.

"You didn't, did you? Were there any others?"

Donovan sighed. "Yours, of course. And, an unknown."

Knowles watched as the two men drank their coffee. "Can I warm it up?" he asked as he reached for the coffee pot.

"I'm good," Fritz told him.

Donovan held out his cup while Knowles topped it off with more coffee.

Knowles set the pot down and stared at Donovan, thinking.

"What?" Donovan asked.

"How long has it been since Frank died?" Knowles asked.

"A couple of months, I guess."

"And, how long since you searched my bar?"

"A few days. What are you getting at, Jimmy?"

"Did it ever occur to you that the box of poison your men took from here had just been opened? That it was a new box of rat poison?"

"What are you saying, Jimmy?" Fritz asked.

"There wasn't a lot of poison left in the box of rat poison that was here on the day that Frank died. The box you took from here when you searched this place was new. I finished that other box off a while back."

Donovan looked confused. "What are you getting at?"

"I'm saying that Stiverson's prints wouldn't be on the box you took because he hasn't worked here since the day Frank died. He's been in since then for a few drinks, but that's it."

Donovan slowly set his cup down on the bar and stared at Knowles. "Are you fucking kidding me? Why didn't you say something before now?" he asked, obviously angry.

Knowles shrugged. "I'm not getting paid to do your job."

"I imagine you threw the old box in the garbage," Fritz said.

Knowles smiled. "I did not. I'm not an idiot. I wrapped it securely in plastic, sealed it, and dropped it off at our local hazardous waste center along with a few other things. Those are the rules, and I follow them. From that point on I have no idea what happened to it."

Donovan turned to Fritz. "Let's go."

"You want the address?" Knowles asked them grinning.

"I know where it's at."

Donovan looked over at Fritz who was sitting in the front passenger seat. "Call the waste center and ask if it's still there."

"You think they will know that? I mean, it's not like they know where every piece of waste that's brought in is located. Or, it may be gone already. This whole thing is a waste of time."

"Maybe it is but. . . Just call, will you?"

"This is ridiculous. There's no way that box is gonna be there." He braced himself as Donovan took a corner. "Slow down, Bobby, you're gonna get us killed."

Donovan glanced down at the speedometer and backed his foot off the accelerator. "Sorry."

"Turn left at the next corner." Fritz watched Donovan start to make a right turn and yelled, "I said left. And, calm down, for God's sake.

"You know what it means if we find that box, don't you?"

"The waste center is right here," Fritz commented. "On your left."

"If we find that box and Stiverson's prints are on it, we've got McKnight's killer," Donovan declared as he pulled the squad car over and parked in front of the building.

Fritz reached for the door handle, then turned and stared at Donovan. "Not really, Bobby. All it will prove is that he touched the box. It won't prove that he killed McKnight."

"He was working the morning Frank died. He was the only one at the bar who could have poisoned him. It's him. I know it is. Let's go," Donovan said as he got out of the car.

"Take a breath, will you? For God's sake, you're gonna give yourself a fucking heart attack."

Donovan grinned. "Am not. Come on, man. Let's go. Time's a-wasting."

"You need a Xanax, Bobby?"

Donovan gave him a puzzling look. "You take that shit?"

Fritz grinned. "No, but I'm about to start 'cause you're driving me fucking nuts."

Thirty minutes later Donovan and Fritz were on their way back to the precinct.

"Well, didn't that go well?" Donovan said sarcastically after a few moments of silence.

"What did you expect? It's a hazardous waste facility. Did you actually think they were going to let you start digging through all that crap to try to find a box? There are regulations about that, you know. Anyway, I told you so."

"I told you so," Donovan repeated, mimicking Fritz.

Fritz grinned. "Well, I did. Anyway, there's nothing you can do about it now. You'll just have to wait until they check it out and get back to you."

35

Officer Chesterton looked over at the door as Donovan walked in. "Morning, Donovan. You're late."

"You keeping tabs on me now, Chesterton?"

"Hey, I'm sorry. It's just not like you, that's all."

"I had a long night."

"With a lady?"

"I wish. What's going on?"

"The report you've been waiting for regarding that rat poison is on your desk," Chesterton told him.

"About damn time. They found that box almost two weeks ago."

"You know these things take time. It's not like yours is the only case they're working on."

Ignoring Chesterton's remark, Donovan walked over to his desk and picked up the report. He shook his head and muttered, "Good."

Detective Fritz glanced over at him. "They found Stiverson's prints," he stated.

"You looked at the report?" Donovan asked.

"I did. I thought you'd be more excited about it."

"You were right when you said it wouldn't prove anything if Stiverson's prints were on the box."

"Thanks. So, where do you go from here?"

Donovan frowned and sat down behind his desk. "I haven't got a clue, Fritz.

"I'm sorry, Bobby. I know how much you want this guy. Do you think that report is enough to get a search warrant for his house?"

Donovan looked at him and shrugged. "Hell if I know. Besides, what would we find there that we could use?"

"I have no idea, but you don't know what the guy might be up to. It might be worth a try."

"We haven't got anything to go on except a few prints. Getting a search warrant on that alone is a real long shot." Donovan thought for a moment, then picked up the phone. "But, you're right. It can't hurt to try. Let's see if the district attorney is in a generous mood this morning."

"And, smile, will you? You've been moping around here for two weeks now. The world isn't going to end if Stiverson's not your man, you know."

"That's not it," Donovan told him. "It's M. J. I haven't seen her for a while."

Fritz looked surprised. "What happened? Did she break up with you?"

"Not exactly. She just wants to cool it for a while."

Fritz stared at Donovan for a moment. "What did you do, Bobby?"

"Nothing. At least, not that I can think of."

"Did you forget her birthday? Say something stupid? That's probably it. You said something stupid, didn't you?"

"Hell, man, how would I know? Do you know what women are thinking? I sure as hell don't"

"Fritz laughed. "No man does, you idiot. What did you do?"

"I mentioned something about her mom being involved with Knowles and she blew up. She told me that once I got my head on straight and figured out that her family had nothing to do with killing her dad, I should give her a call. I didn't even say anything about that. She just got all nasty and. . ."

"I told you to stay away from that subject, didn't I? Didn't I tell you to step away from this whole damn case or it was going to go bad for you?" He stared at Donovan. "Well? Didn't I?"

"All right," Donovan yelled. "You were right! Do you feel better now?"

"I do." He grinned. "Listen, I'm sorry. I didn't mean to get you all pissed off."

Donovan sighed. "Forget it." He picked up the phone. "I'm gonna see if the D. A. will give me that warrant."

Six hours later, Donovan and Fritz were back at the 3rd Precinct having coffee.

"Well, it's something," Fritz declared.

"Something?" Donovan exclaimed. "The man's a damn crook. We've got enough to put him away for years."

"I wonder where he is," Fritz said.

"We've got every cop looking for him. He's bound to be picked up by one of them. God, I can't wait to question him."

"I wonder how long he's been dealing. He has no record, you know."

"Collin, I don't care if it's a day or twenty years. We got him."

Fritz glanced at him, a surprised look on his face. "Do you realize that's the first time you've ever called me by my first name?"

"I did? Sorry, man, it won't happen again."

"You know I hate that name," Fritz told him.

"I said I'm sorry. Drop it. Okay?"

"Just don't let it happen again," Fritz told him.

"How many of those guns do you think are hot? He

hasn't got a gun registration, so he didn't buy any of them legally."

"I'd say most likely all of them. Seven guns is a lot of firepower. What the hell do you think he wanted them for?"

"He's dealing drugs, Fritz. He's probably working with some pretty bad people." Donovan sat back in his chair. "What do you think the dollar amount is?"

"For the drugs?"

"Yeah."

Fritz shrugged. "It was one hell of a bust, Bobby. Probably one of the biggest I've seen since I became a cop. I'd guess around close to a mil."

"Maybe. I don't think it's that much, though. We'll find out soon enough. It won't be long before forensics is done checking everything out. Whatever it is, it's gonna be big." He smiled. "That was a good idea you had to search his house. All in all, it was a good day, Fritz."

"It sure was, Donovan."

"I'm gonna call M. J."

Fritz let out a moan. "Do you think that's a good idea?"

"No. But, I'm going to anyway. I want to tell her about Stiverson. Maybe, with this new information, her insurance company won't have to make that big payout after all."

"It's your life, Donovan. I'm going home to a nice hot homemade dinner."

"Do you like being married?" Donovan asked him.

Fritz grinned. "Most days." He stood up and walked towards the door. "See you in the morning."

Donovan waited until Fritz had gone before he

called Marla Jo. He was about to hang up when she finally answered her phone.

"Donovan? I asked you not to call me."

"I miss you, M. J. I really do.

Marla Jo sighed. "I miss you, too."

"Then why don't you want to see me?"

"I do want to see you. But, everything that's been going on is. . . I don't know, Bobby. I need some time to think about it. You know, to sort it all out and get my head right. First, dad's killed and we don't know who did it, and then you accuse my nephews, and then my mother, and. . ."

"I never accused your mom, M. J.," Donovan said, interrupting her.

"You kinda did, Donovan. And, then this thing with you and me. I think maybe we moved too fast."

"Marla Jo, I've known you for years. The fact that we recently connected on a different level is a good thing."

"I don't know, Bobby. I've got to sort out my feelings."

"I see," Donovan said. "Do me a favor, will you?

"What's that?"

"While you're sorting out your feelings, will you remember one thing?"

"What's that?"

"That I love you."

"You do? Really?"

Donovan laughed. "Really."

"Well, I love you, too."

Donovan sighed. "Thank God. I'm glad we finally agree on something."

"Now what do we do?" Marla Jo asked him.

"I'm starving. Do you want to get something to eat?"

"Yes, please. Come get me."

"I'm on my way."

"Hurry."

36

"I'm telling you for the last time, I didn't kill that bastard. I don't care how many times you ask me, my story isn't going to change."

Fritz stared at him from across the table. Stiverson was wearing him down. He'd been going at it for hours, trying to get Stiverson to confess to killing Frank McKnight.

Stiverson looked away and yawned. "How about a cup of coffee? I could use something to keep me awake."

Fritz pushed his chair back from the table, stood up, and walked out of the room. He glanced over at Donovan, who was at his desk on the phone.

Donovan looked up and motioned for him to come over to him. He hung up the phone and grinned. "You look like crap," he told Fritz.

"Thanks."

"Who's watching him?"

"Patterson is in there with him. It's your turn with Stiverson."

"Has he asked for an attorney yet?" Donovan asked.

"Nope. He's treating this whole thing like it's a big joke. He says he has no idea how the guns and drugs got into his house. We've got his prints all over the stuff and he's sitting there denying he's ever seen it. He said he's going to sue us for harassment and for planting that stuff in his house. The man's nuts and he's driving me crazy."

"You do need a break. I'll go in for a while."

"He's not going to talk, Donovan. It's a waste of time. We've read him his rights. He hasn't asked for legal counsel and he obviously isn't going to admit to anything."

"Did he explain why his prints are on the box of rat poison?" Donovan asked.

"Oh, yeah," Fritz replied. "We put those there, too,"

"Go get some coffee. I'll finish up in there."

"That's the other thing. He wants me to bring him some coffee. He needs something to stay awake."

Donovan grinned. "He's really gotten under your skin, hasn't he?"

"I hate that man," Fritz said, as he looked Donovan in the eyes. "We're never going to prove he committed that murder, you know."

"I figure you're right. Still, with what we've got on him, he will be going away for a long time. In the meanwhile, I'm gonna keep working the McKnight case until I do have enough proof to charge Stiverson with his murder."

"What if he didn't poison McKnight, Bobby? He may be telling the truth."

"Well, if that turns out to be the case, I'm gonna keep looking until I find out who did it. Now, get out of here and go home. I'm gonna go lock up our friend for the night."

"He's no frickin' friend of mine," Fritz said angrily.

"Home. Now!" Donovan said.

Twenty minutes later, Donovan walked into Interrogation Room Six holding a cup of coffee.

Stiverson picked his head up from off the table and grinned. "Sending in the big guns, huh? And, with coffee. Thanks, man. That smells great."

"You look tired, Richard."

"It's been a long night." He reached for the coffee.

Donovan took a sip. "It not only smells great. It tastes great. Good and strong. This should keep me awake for a few more hours."

Stiverson glared at him. "I get it. I don't get any coffee."

"Well, here's the thing. If we give you coffee, it's gonna make you wanna pee. Then, we'll have to undo your cuffs, someone will have to escort you to the john and wait while you pee, and then have to bring you back and.... Well, you get the idea. It's a hassle. So, no, you don't get any coffee."

Stiverson slouched down in his chair and looked away. "Fine!"

"Unless, of course, you want to tell me why you poisoned Frank McKnight. You confess to that and you'll not only get coffee – well, Richard, you'll also get a whole meal to go with it. Your choice. Steak and eggs with toast and. . ." Donovan didn't finish his sentence.

"And, what?" Stiverson asked.

"All the coffee you can drink. So, what's your choice? Confess and eat or have me take you back to your cell?"

"You're a real prick, Donovan."

"I've been called worse."

"I'm sure you have. I'm telling you for the last time. I didn't murder McKnight and I'm tired of this crap. Just take me back to my cell, 'cause I'm done talking to you. Got it?"

"How long have you been dealing drugs?"

"I've never. . ."

"Don't even start," Donovan interrupted. "We found just a little over four pounds of heroin in your house, Stiverson. That makes the street value around

$600,000.00 to $700,000.00. It's a felony, my friend. You are never going to see the light of day again. The gun charges aren't even important. We don't even care about that. The drugs are enough. Do you see where I'm going here? Your life is over. You're going directly to jail. You're not gonna pass go and you're not going to collect one and a half million dollars from the insurance company." Donovan sat back and took another sip of his coffee. He smacked his lips and grinned. "You want some coffee?"

Stiverson glared at him.

"Man, if looks could kill, you could have just stared at McKnight and he would have keeled over. You wouldn't have had to use poison, that's for sure. Anything you want to say?" He waited. "No? Okay. We're done here."

"Wait," Stiverson said as Donovan started to stand up.

Donovan sat back down and looked over at Stiverson. "What?"

"Hypothetically speaking, what kind of a deal could I get on the drug charge if I told you who did kill McKnight?"

Donovan sat back and thought for a moment. "I could talk to the D. A. and see what she has to say. If what you're saying is true, you'd have to have some proof to show her, 'cause just your word isn't worth shit."

"I wasn't working the morning Frank was poisoned. It was Alex Hoffman. He was filling in for Knowles. Jimmy asked me to work and I was going to, but something came up and I asked Alex to do it. We never told Jimmy we made the switch. I wasn't there that morning, Donovan."

"Really," Donovan replied, trying to look surprised. "Well, what about the time cards? Didn't Knowles notice that Hoffman punched in and not you?"

"Hoffman punched in using my card. I paid him cash after Jimmy paid me. So, near as I figure, it had to be Hoffman who did it."

Donovan grinned. "Nice try." He stood up and walked to the door and opened it. "Officer Bailey, would you be kind enough to escort Mr. Stiverson to his cell? I'm done with him." He turned to Stiverson and shook his head. "That was the best you could come up with? Just for your information, Stiverson, Hoffman was having his gall bladder removed when McKnight was poisoned. God, you're so pathetic."

Stiverson stared at him. "I want to call my lawyer," he finally told Donovan. "Now! Give me my phone."

"Well, that took you long enough," Donovan told him. He turned to Bailey. "He's entitled to a phone call. As soon as he's done, take him to his cell."

"Will do," Bailey said.

"And, Bailey?"

"Yes?"

"Make sure you get his phone back."

37

"Are you saying that you may never find out who killed my dad?"

"No, M. J., that's not what I said. I said that right now – notice the 'right now', please – we don't have any evidence that Stiverson killed your dad."

"What about his fingerprints on that box of rat poison you found at that waste place?"

"Not even close to being enough for an arrest. And, even if it was accepted as evidence, a good prosecutor would have it thrown out in seconds. However, right now we've got him on the drug charges and that's enough to send him away for the rest of his life."

Marla Jo looked away and stared out the window.

"What is it? You look bothered."

"Well, Bobby, I am – kinda. Until you find out who killed my dad that means that my entire family will continue to be suspects. Am I wrong?"

"You are wrong. Everyone in your family has been taken off the list. No worries, M. J."

"Is mom off the list, too?"

"Why would you ask that? Of course, she is," Donovan replied.

Marla Jo shrugged. "I don't know. I just get the feeling that you still think she had something to do with it."

"Well, I don't. The rat poison came from the bar. We're pretty sure about that. Please, stop worrying. Your family is in the clear. Okay?"

Marla Jo smiled. "Okay." She looked out the front window of the car. "Do you remember how to get to my mom's house?"

Donovan looked over at her and grinned. "I'm a cop. Of course, I remember."

Marla Jo rolled her eyes. "Well, excuse me. I forgot who I was with for a minute."

"You're excused."

"Oh, I almost forgot," Marla Jo exclaimed. "You'll never guess what I did yesterday."

Donovan smiled. "M. J., if I spent the rest of the day guessing, I'd never get it. What did you do yesterday?"

"I went over to my grandma's and she taught me how to make bread pudding. It is so good, Bobby. No, not good. It's delicious. We're having it for dessert today."

Donovan stared at her looking horrified. "God, no!" he joked. "Tell me it isn't true."

"Car! Bobby, look out!" Marla Jo yelled.

Donovan pulled his car to the right, getting back into his lane, and missing an oncoming car by inches. "Whoops. Sorry."

Marla Jo put her hand over her heart and let out a big breath. "Damn, Bobby, keep your eyes on the road, will you? You scared the crap out of me. You are the worst driver I know. Damn!"

"I said I was sorry."

"You can't be looking around like that when you're driving. We could have been killed. God, I'm shaking."

"Will you stop overreacting? It wasn't that close," Donovan declared.

"Yes, it was. Here, feel this," she said as she reached for his hand and placed it on her left breast. "Feel how hard my heart is beating."

Donovan started to rub her breast. "I better check the other one, too," he said grinning. "You know, to make sure they're both the same size."

Marla Jo took his hand off her breast. "You know they aren't."

"Maybe I should play a little more with the left one. It might grow and then you'd have a perfectly matched pair. Whataya think?"

"How about we just finish our ride in silence?"

"Fine with me."

"My bread pudding is delicious," she said after a few moments.

"We're here," Donovan told her two minutes later as he pulled over and parked in front of McKnight's house. "Good thing, too. That silence was starting to get to me."

Marla Jo looked at him and shook her head. "I don't know what I see in you."

"There's one thing I have to ask before we go in, M. J."

"What's that?"

"Are we seriously having that pudding stuff for dessert?"

"It's called bread pudding and, yes, we are," she replied.

"And, did you honestly make it?"

"I did. She showed me how." She looked at Donovan. "Why the third degree? I can guarantee that there is no poison in it."

"And, you followed the recipe?"

"Of course. I made it exactly like grandma makes it."

"Uh-huh."

Marla Jo stared at him. "What?"

"Well, I was wondering which one of her recipes you used. The one with or without dog poop," he said, laughing, as Marla Jo punched him on the arm. "Ow! That hurt."

"It looks like we're the last to arrive," Marla Jo told Donovan as they walked up the stairs to the front door.

"Do you think your sister has forgiven me yet?"

"She'll be fine. Everyone will be fine."

Donovan took a deep breath and let it out.

Marla Jo grinned. "You're nervous."

"I am not. It's just that there is something about coming here that gives me this weird feeling."

"Like what, Bobby?"

Donovan laughed. "It's nothing. Just forget it. Let's go in." He grabbed her arm and stopped her. "Wait. Are we celebrating something I should know about? A birthday or something?"

Marla Jo took his hand and squeezed it. "Relax, will you? It's just a Sunday dinner get-together. And, I'm sure there will be plenty of wine to help get you through it."

"Just keep those boys out of the kitchen, okay?"

"You're late," Charlotte declared as Marla Jo and Donovan walked into the living room.

Marla Jo glanced at her watch and noticed that they were early by five minutes. "Sorry."

"Well, next time try to get here on time, will you?"

Donovan looked at Marla Jo and frowned. "Are we late?" he mouthed.

She shook her head no. "Are Suzy and mom in the kitchen?" she asked.

"Move," Pete and Mark both yelled at her.

"You're blocking the TV," Pete told her.

"Sorry. Geez, I'm glad everyone is in such a good

mood. Come on, Bobby, let's go say hi to mom."

"Wait," Charlotte called out. "I need to talk to you." She got up off the couch and walked towards the dining room.

Marla Jo shrugged and followed her. "Come on, Bobby. Grandma wants to talk to us."

"The table looks nice," Donovan said, as he walked into the room and looked around. "The table is set for ten. Who else is coming?" he asked Charlotte.

"That's what I wanted to tell you before you went into the kitchen. There's another person here for dinner. Your mother has a guest – a man guest."

"Is it someone I know?" Marla Jo asked.

"I don't think you know him but I'm pretty sure that you do," she said, looking at Donovan.

"What's going on, Grams? And, why is everyone in such a bad mood?"

Charlotte hesitated. "I like you Detective but. . ."

"Please, it's Robert or Bob or Bobby. Take your pick but stop calling me Detective. Okay?"

"Of course. Anyway, as I was saying, I like you and. . ." She hesitated. "Well, I think Betsy likes you, but the rest of the family. . ." She looked away for a moment. "Well, they don't like you," she blurted out. "I'm so sorry, but you thought one of us killed Frank and, well. . . Well, they are still upset about it. I'm sorry."

"What are you saying, Grams? You want us to leave?"

"It might be for the best if you do. I'm so sorry, but I don't want you to be uncomfortable, Robert. You know, with everyone being in such a bad mood and all."

"This is bullshit," Marla Jo exclaimed. "Bobby was just doing his job and we're not going anywhere." She turned and looked at Donovan. "Right?"

Donovan shrugged. "I don't know. Maybe your grandmother is right and we should leave. We can visit your mom another time."

"No." Marla Jo turned and walked towards the kitchen.

"Wait," Charlotte called out. "I lied."

Marla Jo turned back towards her grandmother and stared at her. "What do you mean – you lied?"

"Everyone is upset because of your mother's guest not because of Robert. They don't like it because he's here."

"For God's sake, Grandma, who is it, and what is going on?"

"Your mother has been dating him ever since your dad died. Your brothers and sister think it's too soon, that's all."

"Is it Jimmy Knowles, Charlotte?" Donovan asked.

"How can you possibly know that?" Charlotte asked, looking surprised.

"He was a person of interest when we were looking into Frank's death. He mentioned that he knew Betsy from the past. Plus, he told me they've been dating."

"Mom's dating Jimmy Knowles and you knew it?" Marla Jo inquired.

"Like I said, it came up during the investigation."

"Why didn't you tell me?" Marla Jo asked, starting to get upset.

"It wasn't relevant. Besides, I knew you'd get upset. Which you are."

"She's my mother, Bobby. You should have told me."

"No. It wasn't my place to tell you. If she wanted you

to know, I figured she should be the one to tell you."

"Did you know about this, Grams?"

"None of us knew that she's been dating until today, Marla Jo. That's why everyone is on edge. Well, I'm not. I think it's great. He was a nice boy back then and he still seems like a pretty nice guy. If he makes her happy, I'm all for it. Your mother deserves a little happiness, don't you think."

"I'm sorry I got upset, Bobby. You probably did the right thing by not saying anything to me."

"They dated each other in high school, you know," Charlotte said.

"I know, Grams. Mom just told me about that," Marla Jo told her.

"They were sweethearts years ago and now they're sweethearts again. We figured they'd get married, but he went off to the Army or Navy. I forget which, but that's not important. And, now, all these years later, here they are together again. It's funny how things worked out, isn't it?"

Marla Jo stared at Donovan. "Is it?" she asked.

"What?"

"Funny how things worked out," she stated, looking at him skeptically."

"Hey, that's life. You never know what's gonna happen."

"Or, did they have a little help?" Marla Jo asked him, smiling.

Donovan smiled back at her. "How would I know? Come on. Let's go say hi to your mom and sister," he said, as he took her hand and started walking toward the kitchen.

"And, Jimmy. Let's not forget Jimmy," Marla Jo

added. She turned and looked at her grandmother. "Exactly why didn't you want us to stay for dinner? Is it because you didn't want Bobby to see that Jimmy Knowles is here?"

"Is it really important?" Charlotte asked.

"It is, kinda," Marla Jo said.

"I figure it's because I suspected him of Frank's death knowing he still cared for your mother. But, then, I suspected a lot of people. I think Charlotte thought it might be awkward for us all to be together. Is that right, Charlotte?" Donovan said.

"Well, I knew you'd talked to Jimmy and I don't know what your feelings are about him."

"Jimmy and I are good. No worries. And, if it makes you feel better to hear it, neither Jimmy nor Betsy is on my suspect list. I figure I'll be working this case until I retire because right now my only suspect is Richard Stiverson. And, I've got nothing there. Now, don't you think it's about time we said hello?" He started walking towards the kitchen.

"Oh, Robert?" Charlotte called out.

He turned and looked at her. "Yes?"

"Did our Marlie tell you that she made the dessert for today?"

Donovan smiled. "She mentioned it on the way over here. Is it safe to eat?"

"Oh, my yes," Charlotte told him, grinning from ear to ear. "This pudding is perfectly safe. It's pf bread pudding."

Donovan looked at Marla Jo. "What the hell is pf bread pudding?" he asked.

Marla Jo shrugged and glanced at Charlotte.

Charlotte laughed. "You're the detective, Robert.

You figure it out."

About the Author

I was born in Idaho in 1939. My father's job demanded that we frequently move and, by the age of ten, I had lived in Idaho, Montana, Colorado, Michigan, and Wisconsin.

I am the proud mother of three wonderful sons and two fantastic grandsons. I have no plans to acquire another husband, as they are just too much work.

For most of my life, I worked as an accountant. Two years before I retired, I did a complete switch in careers and managed two Curves fitness facilities in Illinois. I retired in 2002 and moved to Branson, MO. In 2012, I moved to Indiana to be closer to my family and have resided in Highland since then.

I enjoy a good laugh and figure it's my sense of humor that keeps me going when times are tough. Reading has always been one of my passions and I still read a couple of books a week.

In 2014, I wrote my first book, *Blueberries and Bears and My Brother's Shoes*, a book about growing up in the forties and fifties. After I self-published it and gave it to friends and family to read, they encouraged me to get serious about my writing.

I never thought that, at the age of 76, I would become an author. I set a goal for myself to write at least ten books before I die. I've made the ten plus and I'm pretty sure I have a lot more novels kicking around in this head of mine.

I certainly am enjoying my retirement knowing, when I get up each morning, I have something to look forward to. You can find out more about me and my books at www.susanlpare.com. Please visit me there, sign up to be on my readers' list, and feel free to send me your comments.

www.ingramcontent.com/pod-product-compliance
Lightning Source LLC
Chambersburg PA
CBHW050735230626
47052CB00002BA/215